BRING HOME THE MURDER

The Tales of a Tenacious Housesitter

Home Sweet Murder

Home for the Murder

Bring Home the Murder

BRING HOME THE MURDER

Theresa M. Jarvela

NORTH STAR PRESS OF ST. CLOUD, INC.

St. Cloud, Minnesota

This book is dedicated to those who enjoy reading about Meggie's housesitting adventures as much as I enjoy writing about them.

First Edition: September 2015

Printed in the United States of America.

Published by
North Star Press of St. Cloud, Inc.
P.O. Box 451
St. Cloud, Minnesota 56302

www.northstarpress.com

CHAPTER 1

BABY-BOOMER MEGGIE MOORE squeezed a wedge of lemon into her iced tea. "Molly plans to leave for North Dakota at the beginning of July to visit Michael." She sat back against the cushioned booth in Pine Lake Café and glanced out the window. The small town of Pine Lake bustled with tourists. "She'll return to Minnesota by the end of the month."

"I can't believe you're actually going to do it." Shirley Wright grimaced and straightened her cherry-red top across her wide girth. "Just when I think you can't get any wackier, you do something beyond wacky. I seriously wonder about you."

Meggie's lean frame stiffened. She set her drink down and looked at her longtime friend. Shirley's short stature contradicted her vocal abilities. "What do you mean you don't think I'm actually going to do it? I gave them my word." Meggie picked up her paper napkin and opened it to dab her mouth. "Michael's been working in North Dakota for months. It's not easy for either of them being apart so long. They need this time together. Besides, housesitting their hobby farm will be a dream come true."

"You and your word." Shirley clicked her tongue. "I've known you for how many years?"

"Too many to count, I'm afraid." Meggie's lips curled. "I lost track somewhere between a lot and too many." Meggie tucked a scattering of highlighted tendrils behind her ear. She recalled the first time they met, their high school years together and their first gray hairs.

Audrey Peterson, petite and unassuming, looked from Meggie to Shirley and giggled. "You two are such fun. Your friendship is definitely one of a kind."

"Miss Goody Two-Shoes never goes back on her word. You could get out of it if you wanted to." Shirley looked at Audrey for support.

Audrey, not usually one to get involved, smiled at Meggie. "Shirley could be right. You might find it uncomfortable if . . ."

"If the house is haunted?" Meggie rubbed the back of her neck. "I'm not sure I believe in ghosts. Besides, if Molly believes the house is haunted, it doesn't seem to bother her, and as for Michael, he's on the fence about it." She looked at both her friends. "I promised the Rileys I'd housesit, and that's what I intend to do."

"I can see it now." Shirley raised her hand palm out and moved it from one side to the other. *Eccentric Baby-boomer Frightened to Death—Ghost Suspected.* Shirley added extra sugar to her iced tea, gathered the empty packets together and leaned forward. "I think that husband of yours needs to keep you on a short leash. Before you or somebody else gets hurt."

Meggie raised her eyebrow. "Short leash? Believe me, Walter's tried. Unfortunately for him, I never learned to heel."

Shirley stirred her tea and took a sip. "Well, lose my phone number if you get scared out of your wits. I've risked my life more than once for you, and I have no intention of any more repeat performances. BFF or not." She flicked a crumb off her ample bosom and chuckled. "I would love to hear what your hubbie has to say about your next little adventure. I bet he doesn't even know about it."

"HOUSESITTING A HOBBY FARM? At your age?" Walter, slightly overweight, crossed his arms and leaned against the kitchen counter. He glared at Meggie. "What are you thinking?"

She opened her mouth to speak but he cut her off. "Oh, that's right. I forgot. You don't think."

"Walter, just listen."

"I never approved of your harebrained idea to housesit for extra money in the first place. You know that. But did you consider my feelings?"

"Walter, please."

"Three housesitting jobs, three murders. No, let me correct that." He held up four fingers. "Four murders. I forgot you doubled up on that last housesitting adventure and set a record."

He shook his head. "My gosh, Meggie. You barely escaped with your *life* the last time. Not to mention the lives of your sidekicks. But you just keep on truckin'." Walter carried his coffee to the kitchen table and sat down. He rubbed the bridge of his nose. "Don't you want us to enjoy our golden years together?"

Meggie wiped her hands on the dish towel, sat down next to him and took his hand. She had never seen her husband so frustrated. "What could possibly go wrong on a hobby farm?"

Walter's eyes grew round. "With you involved—anything and everything."

"Hon, do you remember how good it felt when you started your bucket list?" She paused. "That bucket list gave your life purpose, didn't it?"

Walter squirmed in his chair, then nodded slightly.

"Shouldn't I have the right to a bucket list?" In a softer voice she added, "You know I've always wanted to live on a hobby farm. At my age, this is the closest I'll ever get to that dream. It's only for a month."

Walter didn't say anything right away. Then he straightened his back and smiled at his wife. "I suppose you deserve to live out your dreams, too." He patted her hand. "And if it's your dream to wake at the crack of dawn, feed the chickens, slop the hogs and shovel manure, who am I to stop you from living that dream?"

Meggie ignored Walter's sarcasm and threw her arms around him. "I knew you would understand."

"Besides," Walter whispered in her ear, "you won't be alone out there."

A spark of hope flitted inside her. She leaned back and looked him in the eye. Had he changed his mind about joining her on the farm? "What do you mean?"

Walter grinned, raised his camouflage-colored coffee mug and winked. "The place is haunted, right?"

THE BELL TINKLED ABOVE THE DOOR at Hearts and Flowers Gift Shop in downtown Pine Lake. Meggie stepped inside and glanced at her wrist watch. To her surprise she had made record time.

"Good morning, dear. You're early." Vera Cunningham, a spry gray-haired lady in her seventies, stood behind the till and glanced up at Meggie. "It was so good of you to come in this morning and help out." Her pen scratched across a note pad. "I know I didn't give you much notice. I would've understood if you couldn't make it."

Meggie smiled and held her hand up. "That's perfectly fine. I didn't have any plans for today. Walter left the house early, and I don't imagine he'll return until late this afternoon."

"Golfing?" Vera closed the till and walked around the counter. Her shoes clicked across the tiled floor. She placed a hand on Meggie's arm and her eyes sparkled. "A man should leave his castle occasionally and enjoy himself."

Meggie slipped off her windbreaker. "I agree. However, his castle has a lawn that needs mowing, and the queen doesn't intend to mow it." She grinned at Vera, walked to the back of the shop and pushed aside the breakroom curtain.

She hung her windbreaker on the coat tree and stepped over to deposit her purse in Vera's desk. A book lay inside the desk drawer. She picked it up. Her brow puckered when she read the title. "I didn't know you were interested in ghost tales, Vera."

4

Vera's eyes darted towards the book. "Would you like a cup of tea before the day begins? I do believe we have time."

"Tea sounds wonderful." Meggie set the book down and closed the drawer. "I didn't have my caffeine this morning. Would you like me to serve the tea?"

"No, you just sit down. Let me wait on you for a change." Vera poured steaming water into a blue-and-white teapot. She reached into the cupboard and took two cups off the shelf.

Meggie sat down at the table and lifted the vase of pink carnations. She sniffed the floral fragrance, positioned the vase in the center of the table, and twisted it until a bright pink carnation faced her.

Vera set two cups of tea on the table and a plate of scones. "I stopped by Swenson's bakery this morning. They have the most delicious orange nut scones." She pulled her chair close to the table and avoided Meggie's eyes. "This organic chai tea's good, don't you agree?"

"It's very good." Meggie waited for a response to her statement but when she failed to receive one said, "Vera, are you avoiding my question?"

Vera set her teacup down. She reached for a scone, broke it in half and brushed the crumbs from her fingers. "Dear, you know I'm not one to interfere in anyone's business."

"I know that." Meggie studied Vera over the rim of her teacup.

"But you see I had good reason to check that book out of the library. I'm not at all familiar with ghosts." She wrinkled her nose. "Truth be told, I don't believe in them."

Meggie bit into her scone and waited for her friend to continue.

"I suppose curiosity got the better of me when you volunteered to housesit at Molly and Michael's hobby farm." Vera patted the corner of her mouth with a napkin. "While I may not believe in ghosts, I thought it a good idea to see if anyone claimed to be injured by them."

Meggie suppressed a giggle and cocked her head. "Are you worried about me?"

"Please don't take this the wrong way, dear." Vera twisted the napkin in her hand. "It's just that I worry about you when you house-sit." She cleared her throat and seemed to have a difficult time continuing. "While I can't foresee anything untoward happening at Molly and Michael's farm, I thought it pertinent to learn all I could about the supernatural."

She looked to Meggie for a response. When there wasn't any, she continued, "I'd then be able to impart the information to you in the unlikely event there's anything to this ghost business of Molly's." Stumbling over her words, Vera quickly added, "And if need be, you'd be prepared to defend yourself."

"I'm sure I'll be fine." Meggie patted Vera's hand. "Besides, to my knowledge ghosts don't hurt people. They just scare the living daylights out of them."

CHAPTER 2

THE MORNING SUN CREPT above the horizon and brightened a world shaded in muted gray. A gentle wind followed. It fluttered the bedroom curtains and feathered Meggie's face. She stirred, her eyes closed but ears tuned to a familiar drone from the other side of the bed. Walter snored like a freight train.

Meggie lifted her head off the pillow and glanced at the bedside clock. Time to get up. She slid quietly out of bed and crept out of the bedroom.

In the kitchen, Meggie poured a cup of coffee and dropped two slices of whole wheat bread into the toaster. She gazed out the window at the backyard. An unfamiliar cat slunk across the dew-covered lawn and stole through the neighbor's fence. Seconds later the neighbor's dog barked, and the feline squeezed back through the fence and ran across the lawn in the opposite direction.

The toast popped up. She spread the slices of toast with raspberry butter and carried her breakfast to the table. While eating she paged through a gardening magazine, read a short article on the care of roses and reveled in the ambience of a quiet summer morning.

The phone rang. She rose from the table and picked up the portable, glancing at the caller ID. She sighed, and her face took on a pinched expression. After several minutes she returned the phone to its cradle. She mumbled to herself and began clearing her breakfast dishes.

After latching the dishwasher door she turned around and almost collided with Walter. He hovered over her. His eyes bulged. Fingers wiggled in the air. "Boo!"

"What do you think you're doing?" She leaned against the counter and crossed her arms.

"I'm saying good morning Casper style." He threw back his shoulders. "Today is your big day. It's off to the farm."

"Does Casper want some breakfast before he floats out the door?" Meggie pecked him on the cheek and moved away from the counter. She opened the refrigerator and reached for the orange juice.

"So what's this you were mumbling about?"

"You know Shirley. She feels it her duty to watch over me like a mother hen. She doesn't like the fact I'm housesitting a house that might be haunted."

Walter chuckled and sat down. "I'm sure she means well."

Meggie spied a container of night crawlers on the second shelf in the refrigerator and tightened the plastic cover with her fingers. "You have to remember to keep the lid locked down on these night crawlers, or we'll have a mess like we did last summer."

"Don't worry about the crawlers. Bill and I plan to feed them to unsuspecting fish the first chance we get. That is, if Shirley lets him out of the house." He paused. "If you can break away from the farm, you and I could take the pontoon out some time next week."

Meggie admitted a pontoon excursion sounded like fun. She joined Walter at the table while he ate his breakfast, and together they made plans for the outing. They talked fish for several minutes. Then Walter changed the subject to the supernatural.

Meggie listened patiently to her husband's ghost stories. When she had enough she rose from the table and positioned herself behind his chair. She placed her index finger in the center of his bald spot and circled the small area with her fingertip.

"What do you think you're doing?" Walter craned his neck and looked up at her.

"I'm checking the crystal ball to see if it predicts ghosts on the hobby farm." She rubbed a little harder. "Nope, no ghosts. Oh, but wait a minute. It does predict Taco Night at the Legion Club will be cancelled if you're late for work."

Walter chuckled and looked at the wall clock. "You're right. I better get out of here." He stood and chucked her under the chin. "You know I'm just trying to give you a hard time."

She pressed her lips together and gave him a curt nod, then rattled around in the cupboard. After locating his camo travel mug, she filled it with coffee and handed it to him. When he couldn't find his Minnesota Twins cap, she pointed to the end of the kitchen table.

Walter flushed. He slapped the cap on his head, bent down and kissed her on the cheek. "Call me tonight after you settle in."

Meggie followed him to the front door and watched him stroll down the walk to his pickup truck. Peppie, their tom cat, crawled out from underneath the truck and meandered up the walk toward the house. The feline sashayed through the front door with his tail in the air, eyed his master, then continued on his way.

LATER THAT MORNING, Meggie sang along to an old Beatles tune and tapped the steering wheel of her Volkswagen Bug. She looked forward to her next adventure. Warm air blew through the driver's window and tossed her hair. She removed a lock from the corner of her eye, tucked it behind her ear and turned the radio up.

The Bug clipped along Highway 52, past several farms, corn fields, and pastures. Meggie admired a ranch-style house hemmed with brightly colored flowers. She watched a small boy barrel out its front door and jump off the porch. He dashed across the yard, a dog in hot pursuit.

A short time later, she turned off the highway and into the small town of Bluff. When she passed St. James Catholic Church, Molly's suggestion sparked her mind. Maybe she would take her young friend's advice, call the chairwoman of the church's summer bazaar and volunteer to help. She might need a bit of distraction from her daily routine at the farm.

Minutes later she left the town of Bluff behind and found herself on a familiar dirt road. She hadn't gone far when the Bug began to shake back and forth on the washboard road. She veered the car to the right and rode the shoulder of the road until the gravel smoothed out.

Soon after, the small yellow farmhouse came into view, nestled against a rolling hill. Meggie slowed the Bug and turned into the long narrow driveway. She pulled up in front of the house and turned off the ignition.

A smile crossed her face when she thought about her bucket list. She might not live on a hobby farm but she could housesit one. She stepped out of the car and stretched her arms.

A rooster crowed from the backyard. It reminded her that Molly had left the fowl in the coop earlier that morning. Her instructions were to let them out when she arrived. But first things first. She opened the trunk of the car, pulled out her luggage and set it on the ground. She reached back in for her brown cowboy boots and closed the trunk.

Meggie pulled the luggage up the front porch steps and wheeled it across the wooden porch floor. She held the screen door open with her hip, fished in her purse for the house key, and slid it into the lock. The door opened into the entryway where subdued light shone from a small window above the staircase landing.

Meggie slung her purse over her shoulder, gripped the cowboy boots with one hand and picked up her suitcase with the other. She carried her baggage through the living room with its fawn-colored furniture and beige walls.

A warm and fuzzy feeling spread over her and she recalled her first visit to the farm. She had expressed to Molly how much fun it would be to housesit where she felt so at home.

The refrigerator hummed in the corner of the combination kitchen and dining area. A warm breeze blew through the open window and lifted the red-and-white-checked café curtains in the air. Several white paper napkins had blown off the kitchen table and onto the floor.

Meggie crossed the sun-streaked floor to the master bedroom. She set her luggage near the end of the double bed, admired the blue-and-white summer quilt, and took out her cell phone.

After a quick text message to Walter to let him know she arrived at the farm, she unpacked her bag. She hung her clothes in the closet and arranged smaller items inside the dresser drawer Molly had emptied for her.

In the kitchen she picked the napkins off the floor and tossed them in the garbage. A notepad with additional instructions lay on the table. She picked it up, read the list over.

Meggie let herself out the back door and headed for the chicken coop. On the way she passed the white gazebo Molly and Michael had built. Tiny compared to her gazebo, the structure stood on a raised platform. A lattice wall about three feet high ran around the entire building. Underneath the roof, yellow woodwork topped each of the supporting beams.

Morning glory vines with blue and white blooms spread over the lattice wall. Hanging baskets sported a brightly colored mixture of sweet-smelling petunias and hung between each section of the gazebo.

Meggie opened the door to the chicken coop and let the fowl out. As she closed the door, her eyes came to rest on a nearby birch tree. The leaves shimmered in the summer sun and eye-like impressions in the bark stared back at her. "Watchful trees" her grandfather used to call them.

A loud snort jolted her mind back to the present. Porky, the young black-and-white boar, stood near the front of the pigpen. Peggy, the sow, wallowed in the sludge by his side. She'd feed them later.

Meggie stepped around the pigpen and walked toward the fence that ran behind the barn. She leaned against the gate, shielded her eyes with her hand and gazed across the back pasture.

In the distance Black, a sleek-coated stallion, grazed near the base of a small hill. His tail swished from side to side. Beauty, a small chestnut-colored mare, stood close by. She dropped her head, then flipped it high and made a full skyward circle with her nose. When the stallion didn't respond to her playfulness, she wandered off toward a wooded area.

Meggie pushed herself away from the gate and made her way back to the house. She didn't have to call the horses in from pasture until later so she had the rest of the day to settle in and make herself at home.

THAT EVENING MEGGIE DRESSED for bed. She carried her toiletries into the master bedroom bathroom and set them on the counter. After brushing her teeth, she smoothed night cream over her face and studied her reflection in the mirror above the sink. She looked tired. It had been a long day and she needed a good night's sleep.

Meggie stepped away from the bathroom counter. She reached for the light switch near the door but her hand stopped mid-air. A faint spicy fragrance tickled her nose. She sniffed again but didn't smell anything odd and convinced herself she imagined it.

Meggie crawled into bed. Exhausted but unable to sleep, she lay awake. Thoughts of the supernatural flashed through her mind. No doubt the result of pointless chatter about ghosts and haunted houses from well-meaning friends and one husband.

Determined to let nothing spoil her stay at the hobby farm, Meggie barred her mind to thoughts of the supernatural and anything negative. She closed her eyes and snuggled between the crispy-clean sheets. But despite her best intentions, tiny cracks developed in her mind's armor and seeds of doubt marched through.

A chorus of frogs sang through the bedroom window. Their croaks mingled together to form a melody. It reminded her of something Walter told her one summer night years ago—when many frogs croak together a strong storm will follow.

Meggie didn't know if it were true or not. It didn't make much difference either way because she enjoyed a good Minnesota storm. Besides, what did a bunch of frogs know, anyway?

CHAPTER 3

THE NEXT EVENING, MEGGIE sat at the kitchen table. She parted the billowing curtains and peered into the black night. All day the weather had screamed storm. In the distance lightning streaked across the summer sky and wind whistled around the small farmhouse.

From the kitchen she watched a tall jack pine sway. Seconds later lightning crackled and thunder rumbled. The farmyard lit up like a Christmas tree. Sheets hung from the clothesline and snapped in the wind. Her favorite crop pants ballooned with air and whipped back and forth.

Seconds later the sky opened. Rain fell in sheets, pounded against the kitchen window and lashed the side of the house. She jumped up, knocking her chair backward in the process. It clattered against the hard oak floor. She reached out and slammed the window shut.

In the master bedroom she shut out the deluge that gusted through the window. Rainwater puddled at her feet. She grabbed a towel from the bathroom and tossed it on the floor to soak up the mess.

Once the windows were secured downstairs she ran to the entryway, switched on the light and vaulted up the staircase to the landing. Rain pummeled the rooftop. It blew through the window screen and dripped down the wall. She shut the window. The farmhouse rattled around her. Then the lights went out.

She felt her way into the first bedroom. A bolt of lightning lit up the room and gave her time to secure the window. The room went black again. She stretched her arms in front of her and slowly made her way into the larger bedroom. She took baby steps to the window. Why hadn't she grabbed a flashlight?

Lightning flashed. Thunder boomed. A squeal rent the air. It came from the backyard. "Oh, no! The pigs are loose!"

Meggie's heart pounded as she stumbled back through the bedrooms and onto the landing. In the dark, her feet inched their way across the top stair. A lightning bolt illuminated the staircase. She darted down the flight of stairs and leapt across the bottom step.

A sharp pain shot through her knee, and she doubled over. She should have known better than to move so fast. Meggie massaged the burning area, then edged her way to the entryway closet. Her hands slid over the door and found the door knob. She reached inside for the flashlight.

Meggie pulled on the front door. It swung towards her. The outside door wouldn't budge against the wind. She braced her shoulder on it, pushed with her legs and squeezed onto the porch. She pressed the flashlight switch but nothing happened. Shook it. Still no light. She set it down, carefully descended the porch steps and headed for the backyard.

Off and on, the sky lit up. Rain hammered her head and flowed down her face. It saturated her shirt and dripped down her back.

"Here piggy, piggy," Meggie yelled above the storm. She waited for a familiar snort but none came. Frantic, her voice raised an octave. "Here piggy, piggy."

Meggie cocked an ear and listened. A faint snort behind one of the lilac trees, then another snort. She grabbed a handful of lilac branches and shook them. "Come out of there," she demanded. Seconds later Porky ambled out from behind the lilac tree with Peggy bringing up the rear.

The pigpen's faint outline stood against the black night. Its gate creaked back and forth. Her face tightened. She had forgotten to lock the pigs inside their sleeping quarters, and they had broken the latch on the gate. Molly had warned her that pigs were great escape artists. She was right.

Meggie waved her arms in front of the animals in an attempt to herd them in the right direction. They darted this way and that. She ran after them, positioned herself behind their backsides and flapped her arms up and down.

"Get in the pen you pigs!"

They snorted, turned around and trotted through the gate.

Meggie followed them into the pen. Her feet sank in the rain-soaked muck. She lost her balance and fell to one knee. She tried to push herself up, but her hands sank further into the sludge-filled hole, and she toppled forward. She cursed under her breath and wanted to cry but couldn't. She raised her head in time to watch the pigs trot past her and back out of the gate.

Meggie had almost given up when she remembered the slop pail sitting on the back patio. She could entice the pigs back inside the pen with food. She trudged slowly back to the house. After pouring the excess water out of the bucket, she went in search of the pigs.

Several minutes later the pigs were inside the pen, lured by a bucket of slop. They waddled into the hut and she slapped the padlock on the kennel gate.

Meggie then sloshed her way to the horses' quarters. She took hold of the wooden board that held the barn door closed, shoved it to the left and pulled on the weathered door. It creaked open. The sweet scent of hay, oiled leather, and an earthy smell wafted through the air. Whinnies rose from the center of the barn and hooves stomped.

Meggie lifted the battery powered lantern off the wall near the barn entrance. She switched it on and strode toward the horse stalls. She held the lantern high as she neared Black's stall. Fear radiated from the stallion's eyes.

"There now, Black." She stroked his nose. In return the big black horse nuzzled her hand. "Don't be frightened." Meggie moved to Beauty's stall and stroked her as well. The horses seemed to calm down.

But time was in short supply and she wasted none of it. She swung the lantern from side to side in front of the stalls and searched for a rope she had seen earlier. She lifted it off the peg and hustled outside.

Meggie hung the lantern from a fence post and uncoiled the rope. She weaved it through the broken pig gate and around the fence post then knotted it. Satisfied that the pigs wouldn't get out of the pen, she wiped her hands against her jean shorts and hurried to the chicken coop. The fowl were safe and sound.

At the back door Meggie tried the knob but found it locked. A groan escaped her. Her clothes were drenched and her body covered in mud. Now the door was locked. She stamped her foot and mud splattered over her.

She turned on her heel, held the lantern in front of her and strode around to the front of the house. After depositing her dirty clothes and shoes in the entryway she made her way into the kitchen. She dried the lantern off and set it on the table.

Meggie grabbed hold of the kitchen chair, set it upright and plopped down before her legs gave out. She wiped her face and squeezed rainwater from her hair. A droplet of water clung fast to the tip of her nose. She shook it off, folded her arms on the table and placed her head in them.

Seconds later her cell phone rang. She snatched it off the table.

"Are you in the basement?" Walter barked. "If you're not, take the cell phone with you and get down there. Now." His voice cut in and out. "A tornado warning . . ."

"Walter, I can't hear you," Meggie shouted into the phone. "Walter?" The word "tornado" reverberated in her mind. She had no time to lose. Cell phone in hand, she grabbed the lantern off the table and hurried toward the cellar door near the back of the house.

She turned the knob and pushed the door open. Holding fast to the stair rail, she held the lantern in front of her and descended the steep uneven wooden stairs.

A dank odor filled the air in the unfinished basement. The light beamed on a dark area half the size of the house. The glow swept over the water heater, cardboard boxes and a wooden crate in the corner of the basement. She ducked her head under the plumbing pipes, maneuvered her way to the corner and sat down on the wooden crate to wait out the storm.

The basement muffled the howl of the tempest. Every few minutes lightning flashed and lit up the ground level window. Objects knocked against its glass. Meggie rested her elbows on her knees and cupped her face with her hands. She still liked summer storms, but not tornadoes. And she hated chasing pigs in the dark.

MUCH LATER, MEGGIE PLODDED up the basement stairs. She halted near the light switch and flipped it with her finger. No power. She closed the basement door then stepped out onto the back patio and held the lantern up.

Energy spent, the storm had moved away. Lightning flashed in the distance, the ferocious winds had blown themselves out, and the pelting rain had turned to drizzle.

Barely awake, she turned to go inside. Her eye caught a movement in the shadows. Translucent and barely visible, the wispy shape swirled near the center of the yard and appeared to float towards her.

Meggie's breath felt constricted. It was difficult to swallow. She backed into the house and closed the door. Had she just witnessed an apparition? She stepped sideways, slowly leaned her head to the side and pecked through the small window near the back door.

Apparition or not, it had disappeared. Only darkened shadows remained in its place. It must have been her imagination, she thought.

The long day had tired her, the storm had scared her, and now her mind played tricks on her.

Meggie shook off her fear and held the lantern in front of her. She moved through the kitchen and into the living room. Nothing appeared damaged. The lantern glowed in the entryway and over the staircase. The steps creaked as she ascended. On the landing she discovered the bedroom door had blown shut. She pushed it open.

The lantern threw shadows against the bedroom walls. She moved on to the second bedroom. Both rooms held no visible damage. As far as she could tell, the entire house had weathered the storm.

Downstairs she set the lantern on the bedside table and sent a text message to Walter and Molly to let them know all was good. She staggered to the bedroom window and opened it to let the fresh air in.

After shedding her underclothes, she tossed them in the hamper and donned a night shirt. Her feet dragged on the way to bed. She threw herself across the mattress, too tired to think or care about anything.

Before she fell asleep, frogs flashed through her mind. Those darn amphibians had been right after all.

CHAPTER 4

THE EARLY MORNING SUN filtered through the lacy bedroom curtains and created patterns across the blue-and-white summer quilt. Meggie stirred under the covers and focused her mind, fuzzy from the early morning hour. Flashbacks of the previous night played inside her head.

She threw back the covers, padded across the room and flipped the light switch. The ceiling light glowed. Relieved, she headed for the kitchen. She checked the contents of the refrigerator and found nothing spoiled. All items in the freezer section were still frozen and didn't appear to have thawed at all.

The kitchen felt stuffy. A strange odor lingered in the air. She sniffed. It smelled like cigar smoke. But that was impossible, she thought. The windows had been closed all night, so naturally the room would be odorous. A little fresh air would work wonders.

She slid the kitchen curtains aside and pushed up on the window frame. She inhaled the fresh outdoor smell. A song bird's trill greeted her. The storm had passed and all was right with the world.

But a closer look out the window told a different story. The large flower pot Molly kept near the back door sat upright under the clothesline. The bright red blooms waved in the gentle breeze.

A crumpled white sheet lay on the ground next to the flower pot and a second sheet dangled above it. Her pants, full of life the night before, were wrapped around the clothesline, the air sucked out of them.

Anxious to see what further havoc the storm had wreaked, she prepared a quick breakfast. While she ate, she listened to the radio to catch any news of the storm. She had just finished her poppyseed muffin when the broadcaster announced there had been considerable storm damage throughout the area but no deaths reported thus far.

Meggie downed the last of her apple juice and headed out the back door. She gasped at the sight that awaited her. No doubt about it. The storm left its calling card.

The outdoor grill leaned precariously against the outside of the house, blown off the back patio. Debris and branches littered the back-yard. The beautiful birch tree lay on its side, a casualty of the storm. The bark's eye-like impressions no longer discernible.

Meggie strode toward the clothesline, picked up the window bird feeder and suctioned it back onto the kitchen window. A long sigh escaped her. The rest of the clean-up would have to wait until later. Right now the animals were her main concern. She prayed they survived the storm.

On her way to the chicken coop, she stopped at the gazebo and peeked in. The wicker chair lay on its side and a puddle of rain-water pooled on the small table. Other than that, there didn't seem to be any damage inside the gazebo. A quick walk around the outside of the building lifted her spirits. The main structure stood fast.

The same couldn't be said for the flowers. The morning glory vines still twisted in and out of the open wall but with fewer blooms. Most of the blue-and-white blossoms had succumbed to the high winds and lay scattered on the ground.

The pretty petunias didn't fare well either. Two hanging bas-kets lay on the ground near the base of the gazebo, their brightly col-ored flowers now dressed in mud. She bent over, picked up the baskets and set them in the sun to dry.

Meggie continued on the path to the hutch. She skirted a water puddle and stepped over a large pine branch. The fowl clucked as the coop door swung open. A quick look inside the building told her all was well. She closed the door before the chickens could get out. They could stay in the coop until the yard inspection was completed.

The pigs snorted from the latched pen and their beady eyes followed her as she hurried past them toward the barn. She shot them a dirty look. After what those pork chops put her through the night before, they could grunt all they wanted. They were going to wait until she was good and ready to let them out.

Nothing seemed amiss inside the barn. Black stood near the front of the stall and bobbed his head when she approached. Beauty stood quietly in the next stall over and acted as though nothing unusual happened during the night.

A slow smile crossed Meggie's face. The animals had survived the storm, the house still stood and she had no lingering effects from the night before. With renewed vigor she set about her tasks.

After the horses were fed and watered, she led them out of the barn and pushed the pasture gate open. Black neighed and tossed his head. He nudged Beauty with his nose then trotted off. The mare nickered, glanced back at Meggie and trotted after him.

Meggie turned away from the horses and strode toward the pigpen. Inside the pen she slipped the padlock off the kennel door and lifted the latch. Porky raised his snout and wobbled past her through the gate with Peggy close behind. They loitered near the trough until it was filled then lowered their snouts and slurped along the bottom of the feeder.

On her return to the house Meggie avoided the usual path and headed for the downed birch tree. The porkers had lucked out. If she hadn't rescued them when she did they might be lying under the toppled tree right now. Their grunts silenced forever.

Meggie inched closer to get a better look at the beautiful birch tree. A lump formed in her throat. What a loss. Yesterday the tree stood tall and its leaves glistened in the sun. Now it would be reduced to firewood.

When the wind and tree collided, the tree met its fate. She pressed her lips together and shook her head. As if in agreement, a small bird perched on a branch of the fallen tree, twitched its head and hopped away.

With a heavy heart, Meggie backed away from the exposed roots and turned toward the lilac bushes. She stretched her leg over the upturned earth and planted it near a large clump of dirt. But when she attempted to lift her other foot, it caught in a tangle of roots. Her body lurched and arms flailed before her foot broke free. She wavered back and forth then toppled face down in the wet grass and soil, nose pressed to the ground.

A sharp pain shot through her arm. She bared her teeth then took a deep breath and mustered enough strength to push onto all fours and into a sitting position. She wiped her dirty hands across the front of her shirt and mopped sweat from her brow.

Blood formed across a scrape on her arm. She brushed the dirt away from the open wound and glanced down at what caused her injury. A chunk of concrete protruded through the exposed tree roots. It tilted precariously

Curiosity aroused, she cleared the intertwined grasses and weeds away from the concrete and sat back on her haunches. Her eyes grew round. The tree roots had pulled the piece of concrete off a slight projection in the ground and exposed a gaping black hole.

Deep lines zigzagged across the top of the cement and several edges had broken away. She removed the loose chunks of concrete and tossed them aside. With her shoulders lowered, she attempted to push the remaining chunk of concrete off its resting place but it refused to budge.

Determined to expose the entire hole, she grabbed both sides of the heavy object, wiggled it back and forth and away from her. After several minutes she let go and caught her breath. She continued wrestling with the piece of cement, but it proved to be a struggle.

Meggie scooted to the other side of the concrete and kept working it. At last the heavy chunk teetered, slid off its resting place and exposed a hole in the earth. It appeared to be about three or four feet wide. An abandoned well? She picked up a small piece of concrete and tossed it into the cavity.

A familiar pain shot through Meggie's lower back. She blew through her mouth and slowly straightened up. Her forehead perspired and the skin beneath her nose grew damp. She wiped her face with her forearm and waited for her heart rate to slow down.

She leaned over the opening to get a better look but felt woozy and angled her body away from the black cavity. The pain in her back throbbed. Once again she had forgotten her limitations.

Molly and Michael would probably want to fill the well with rocks or gravel to avoid any accidents. Until then, it would have to be covered up but she had no intentions of moving the concrete back into place.

Once her equilibrium returned, she peered into the hole for a second time. Weathered wood lined the inside near the top of the well. Bricks covered the wall farther down. Without a flashlight she couldn't tell the well's depth, but judging by the clink of the concrete when it hit bottom, she assumed it didn't go very deep.

While she debated what her next step should be, a gust of cold air rose from the well, enveloped her for several seconds and dissipated. Her brows narrowed and a tingle ran down her spine. She pushed herself away from the edge of the old well and stood up.

The odd incident left her shaken and a bit confused. Ghost thoughts inserted themselves into her mind but she ignored them. A job needed to be done and she had to focus. The sooner the well presented no safety hazard, the better she would feel. She closed her eyes and concentrated. Michael had done some remodeling. More than likely he kept his tools in the garage. With any luck she might find leftover building supplies there as well.

Meggie entered the garage through the side door. She flipped the light switch, located the button to raise the automatic garage door and pressed it. The door groaned and rattled upward.

Sunlight flooded the overstuffed area. Empty flower baskets, bags of starter soil and miscellaneous garden tools lined the wall to her left. Larger gardening implements leaned against the wall.

On the opposite side of the garage two sawhorses sat next to a riding lawn mower. Bricks were piled behind the mower. Further down that side of the garage, various power tools hung over a work bench.

Her hands rested on her hips. She surveyed the room and spotted what appeared to be odds and ends of lumber and planks leaning against the back wall. But she had a problem. How to forge a path through all the clutter to reach them?

Empty cardboard boxes, floor lamps, and a vacuum cleaner were pushed aside on her way through the disordered paraphernalia. Dust swirled in the air. She waved a hand in front of her face to clear it away. She squeezed past an arm chair and found herself in front of the building material.

One by one she pulled the odd-sized pieces of lumber and planks toward her. When she came to a piece of plywood that appeared to be the right size, she slid it out. Holding the top of the plywood, she pushed it toward the front of the garage and leaned it against the door frame.

She located a wheelbarrow behind the garage and wheeled it to the open door. After catching her breath, she walked back inside the garage to collect several bricks. She carried them to the wheelbarrow then slid the piece of plywood over the top of the cart. With the wheelbarrow loaded, she wheeled it to the front porch and parked it.

In the house she filled a water bottle and inserted new batteries in the flashlight then returned to the porch. She set the smaller rocking chair upright and sat down to take a short break. She looked at the mess surrounding her.

Molly's hand-painted flower pot lay broken in half near the edge of the porch, its contents strewn on the ground below. Branches from the weeping willow in the front yard lay scattered about and a bird feeder reclined under the maple tree. She closed her eyes to shut out the disarray.

After a short break she pushed the cumbersome cart to the backyard. She knelt down and stretched out on the ground by the well's edge. With the flashlight at arm's length, she swept it back and forth. Someone had partially filled the well with rocks and gravel.

Meggie set the flashlight down and pushed herself up from the edge of the well. She grabbed hold of the plywood, pulled it over the hole and set the bricks on top of it. She brushed her hands off. That feat accomplished, she wheeled the barrow back to the garage and made a mental note to call Molly to let her know about her discovery.

In the front yard, she collected the large branches from around the trees and disposed of them near the wood line behind the garage. On her way back to the house she picked up the bird feeder and hung it from a branch of the maple tree.

Next Meggie began the front porch clean-up. She carried the broken flower pot to the garbage. After replanting the salvaged flowers in another container, she set the container down on the porch floor. She righted the larger rocking chair and swept the entire area.

LATER THAT AFTERNOON, she lowered herself into the rocking chair. She leaned her head back and tried to rest. But it was not to be. She flinched at a noisy patter close by and opened her eyes. A black squirrel jumped off the porch bird feeder, scampered across the grass and up the maple tree, having located the new home for the bird feeder. Birds flew off when the squirrel took possession.

When the squirrel vacated the bird feeder, a chickadee soared in and lit on it. It picked up a sunflower seed with its beak and flew off. Meggie closed her eyes and thought about all the wild creatures. Where did they hide during a storm?

THAT EVENING AFTER CHORES, Meggie brewed a cup of tea and sat down in front of the television to watch the news. A shooting in St. Paul, another Vikings football player in trouble, and a pile-up along

I-94 during rush hour traffic. Not a good mood setter. The weather report, however, brought a bit of hope for the days ahead.

She turned the channel to one of her favorite evening shows, but found it hard to concentrate. Her mind wandered to the strange occurrences that had taken place since she arrived at the farmhouse —odors unaccounted for, visions in the dead of night, and cold air from an abandoned well. She rubbed her eyes. She was tired, that was it. Everything would look different after a good night's rest.

Meggie attempted to finish the television show, but dozed in the overstuffed armchair. By the time she woke it had grown dark outside. It was late and morning would come early. She stood and straightened her back. It ached from overwork. Would she ever learn?

In the bedroom she stifled a yawn and slipped a nightgown over her shoulders. She shuffled into the bathroom. The scent of Old Spice cologne wafted around her. She froze. Her pulse quickened.

The first time she experienced the strange occurrence she blamed her imagination, but not this time. She reached for the door on the medicine cabinet above the bathroom sink, slid it open and scanned the contents inside.

She pulled the bathroom vanity drawer out and pawed through hair brushes and combs, then dropped to her knees in front of the vanity door. She tugged on it and peered inside.

Shampoos, conditioners, bath oil, and other miscellaneous bath products filled the front portion of the cabinet. She hugged the various sized containers, pulled them out and dumped them on the floor beside her.

Her arms reached inside the cabinet and removed several containers of cleaning products, unopened bars of soap, and bathroom sponges. After the last item had been pulled from the cabinet, she sat back on her haunches and studied the mess on the floor. As much as she willed it, not one Old Spice product existed in that mess.

CHAPTER 5

MEGGIE STRETCHED HER ARMS and glanced at the kitchen clock. She had slept later than planned and would need to hurry if she wanted to finish her chores and get on the road later in the morning.

She called Walter to let him know she would be a little late, then punched in Shirley's number. No one answered her call.

After a quick breakfast, she slipped on a pair of rubber boots, stuck a pair of work gloves in her pocket and set off to do the early morning chores. At the chicken coop she dumped seed into the feeders and filled the water dish then strode toward the barn.

"Good morning, Black." She reached up to stroke his face. Black nuzzled her hand. His large limpid eyes rested on her as she rubbed her cheek against the side of his face. Careful not to tarry, she led both horses out to pasture. She glanced at her watch and wondered how long it would take to muck out the stable.

The work cart was parked inside the barn and loaded with cleaning tools. She pushed it toward the horse stalls and parked it facing the barn door. The first order of business—clean the stalls.

After the droppings were removed and dumped, she grabbed the pitch fork and separated the soiled bedding from the clean bedding. The clean bedding was tossed to the corners of the stall. The dirty bedding thrown in the cart and wheeled outside to the manure pile.

Once the floor had been thoroughly swept and cleaned with a disinfectant, Meggie rested against the stable gate. She brushed the hair out of her eyes and glanced at her watch. It was getting late. She would have to replace the bedding later that day. Tomorrow she would tackle Beauty's stall.

She pushed the cart outside and dumped the last load of old straw and manure, then parked the wheelbarrow inside the barn. She carried the slop buckets to the pigpen and emptied them into the troughs.

Back at the house, Meggie hosed her boots off and sat down on the back patio to catch her breath. She leaned her head back and blew air onto her face. What a workout. It had taken longer and a lot more energy than expected to clean the stall. *You better face it, Meggie. You're not as young as you used to be.*

A crow cawed nearby. It swooped out of a tall jack pine and landed on the ground to scavenge for food. The sight jarred her memory. She hurried into the house, retrieved the bag of old bread ends she brought from home and tossed them into the yard for the black birds.

After a quick shower, Meggie dressed and sat down at the kitchen table to work on her to-do list. She tapped a pen on the notepad and tried to think if she had forgotten anything. After her mind clicked each item off and she couldn't think of anything else, she stuck the list in her purse.

Walter expected her to stop by the house when she arrived in Pine Lake. If everything went as planned, she would have enough time to visit with him, run her errands and possibly meet Shirley at Pine Lake Café for a quick bite to eat.

God's yolk-yellow morning star climbed higher in the sky and radiated a heat that would develop into a scorcher by mid-day. Meggie switched the air conditioning on inside the Bug and started off down the drive.

The horses stood near the pasture fence. Black held his head erect and watched as she drove by. Beauty nibbled grass several yards away and paid no attention. Meggie wondered how horses stayed cool in the summer and warm in the winter. She would have to Google it when she got back to the farm.

Once she reached the highway and could pick up speed, the Bug zipped past familiar landmarks and reached the Mississippi Bridge in record time. There she slowed the car and gazed in wonder at the glistening river and majestic pines huddled along its banks. The mighty Mississippi River meandered on its journey and offered no clues to its force and power.

Minutes later she arrived at her home. Surprised to see Walter in the front yard watering the flower bed, she tooted the horn at him. He turned and waved, then continued to mist the flowers.

"Good morning," Meggie called. She crossed the yard and gave Walter a kiss. Peppie sauntered out from the other side of the flower bed, pranced up to her and wrapped himself around her legs. She bent over and stroked his head. "How's my little tiger this morning? I miss you."

Walter turned the hose off and tossed it on the ground. "Cup of coffee?" When Meggie nodded, he led the way to the front door and followed her into the kitchen. "How's my favorite cowgirl this morning?" He reached into the cupboard for a mug, filled it with coffee and handed it to her.

Meggie thanked him and carried her coffee to the table. "It's going great. The storm challenged me though." She sat down and fingered through the mail lying on the table. "I found an old well in the backyard yesterday."

"What do you mean you found an old well in the backyard?"

"A birch tree behind the house fell during the storm. I went to check it out and stumbled onto the well—literally. I'm not even sure if Michael and Molly are aware it's there. I covered it back up. Molly will have to decide what to do with it when she gets home." Meggie debated whether or not to mention the strange occurrences that took place at the farm and decided against it.

"I can drive out and cut the tree up for firewood," Walter offered. "Michael owns a chainsaw, doesn't he?"

Meggie shrugged and promised to find out. "On another note —I would feel better if Molly had left Brandy at the house."

Walter held his favorite coffee mug in one hand and a plate of chocolate-covered donuts in the other. He set them down in front of his wife and made himself comfortable at the head of the table. "Her black lab?"

"He's a yellow lab." Meggie reached for a donut. "She didn't want to travel with him but Michael misses him so much. She packed him up and took him with her."

"Are you a dog lover now?" Walter's eyes danced, and a smile played about his lips. "Or just a little nervous out there by yourself with only the chickens and pigs to keep you company?" He bit into a donut but his eyes stayed fixed on Meggie. "Or does there happen to be another reason you want the company of a dog?"

"I never said anything about being nervous." Her decision not to confide in Walter about the strange occurrences had been a good one. "I only meant he would have been company for me."

Walter scratched his chin and gave his wife a hard stare. He prodded her to tell him the real reason for her sudden canine interest, but she denied any hidden motive. "I could stay with you at the farm."

"At my age, I don't need a babysitter," Meggie said.

An hour later Walter walked Meggie to the Bug, waited for her to settle into the driver's seat and closed the car door. "You know, a dog might not be a bad idea." He drummed his fingers on the Bug's roof and looked down at her. "You might be able to rent a dog."

"Oh, don't be silly," Meggie smirked while she buckled her seat belt.

"If you change your mind just let me know and I'll see what I can do. You know," he glanced from side to side, leaned close to Meggie and lowered his voice, "some claim dogs can see ghosts."

Meggie rolled her eyes and looked away before she laughed. She didn't want to encourage him.

He tapped her on the shoulder. "But that's not all." He closed one eye and pointed his finger over her head. "They say if humans look right over the top of a dog's head through the space between its ears, they might be able to see them, too." His eyes gleamed and he fluttered his fingers at Meggie. "Boo!"

"Honestly, Walter. You ought to grow up." Meggie turned the key and gave him a piercing stare. "You're just trying to scare me, but it won't work." She shifted her body in the driver's seat, looked out the rear window and backed the car around.

Walter called after her, "And a dog's bark wards off the Angel of Death!"

LATER THAT EVENING, Meggie sat on the front porch. She rocked back and forth and thought about summer nights long ago. Lightning bugs. Whatever happened to them? Across the road firecrackers popped and crackled. Colored fire exploded in the night sky. She had been invited to join the neighbors for their annual fireworks display, but declined. As much as she loved her independence, she wasn't in the mood to celebrate it.

CHAPTER 6

VERA LOOKED UP WHEN MEGGIE entered the shop. "So glad
you're here, dear. Eldon just left for the post office, but he'll
be back shortly. We've had such a busy Monday morning."

Meggie smiled to herself. Eldon's hours had increased dramatically in the last few months since he no longer owned the smoke shop.
She wondered how long it would be until Pine Lake heard wedding
bells. "I think your idea to have a July sale is going to prove successful."

"I do hope you're right." Vera smiled and tore a sticky note off
the pad. She set it on the cash register and walked around the counter
to stand near Meggie. "I won't keep you long today. I know you're
busy on the farm. But tell me, did you enjoy your holiday?"

Meggie shrugged and told Vera about the invitation she received from Donna Jones, a neighbor who lived across the road from
Riley's farm. She admitted she didn't go to the fireworks festivities because she hadn't been in the mood to socialize. Besides, she needed
to recuperate after the storm clean-up.

Vera nodded her understanding and put her hands together.
"Well, I hope you've recovered your strength. Francis Johnson dropped
off a supply of hand painted loons on Friday. Nettie brought me more
crocheted dish towels. Perhaps you can display them? And if you have
time, would you take an inventory of the supplies in the storeroom?"

The bell tinkled above the door and an elderly woman entered
the shop. Vera greeted her by name. She took the older woman's hand
and placed it between her own. "It's so nice to see you, Edith. It has
been far too long." She patted her friend's hand and asked her if she
knew Meggie.

When the elderly woman shook her head, Vera introduced them. "Edith Knutson, Meggie Moore. Meggie helps out at the shop and we've grown very close over the years. I don't know what I'd do without her." Vera turned to Meggie. "Edith and I have known one another for years. I've tried to encourage her to get away from Bluff and visit Pine Lake more often."

Meggie shook Edith's hand. "What a coincidence. I'm so glad to meet you. Molly Riley gave me your name as contact person for St. James's church bazaar. I may have time to volunteer my services." When Edith gave her a quizzical look, she went on to explain. "I'm housesitting at Molly and Michael's hobby farm."

After a few minutes of conversation, Meggie promised to give Edith a call and left the two women alone. She made her way to the storeroom and located the container of hand-painted loons and the box of crocheted dish towels. She carried them to the front of the shop.

By the time she added the finishing touches to the Loon display, Edith had finished her shopping and said her goodbyes to Vera. She waved at Meggie as she left.

A few minutes later, Eldon returned from the post office. He wore his favorite red pullover shirt. A pen stuck out of the pocket. He asked her about Walter and chatted several minutes about the hobby farm before leaving to finish his work.

Meggie set the last crocheted dish towel on the table and stood back. The display looked nice. She collected the container and cardboard box, carried them to the back of the building and returned to the front of the shop.

Vera stood behind the till and set the telephone in its cradle. She whispered something to Eldon then motioned to Meggie. "Would you like a cup of tea? I have some delicious turtle cookies Nettie made for us. Eldon promised to watch over the shop while we ladies take a much-earned break."

Eldon looked guilty. "I confess it took me longer than usual to return from the post office. I ran into an old friend and we decided to have coffee at Pine Lake Café."

Meggie followed her employer into the breakroom. While Vera rummaged in the cupboard, Meggie poured hot water into two cups and placed a tea bag in each. She carried them to the table. "I'm glad to see Nettie's returned to her baking."

"She's feeling much better. You know she suffers from that nasty ulcer." Vera set the plated turtle cookies on the table. "Aren't these cookies delightful? The walnut pieces make the cutest head and legs and the chocolate frosting creates the most adorable turtle shell." She slid her chair close to the table and reached for a napkin. "Well, dear, how are you adjusting to farm life?"

Meggie chuckled, lifted a turtle cookie to her mouth and bit the head off. "I can honestly say it's an experience like no other."

Vera tilted her head. "New experiences definitely make life exciting. I do hope your experiences have been positive."

"For the most part my hobby farm experiences have been positive. I feel close to nature around the animals. I've discovered that roosters crow at different times of the day when I thought they only crowed at dawn. And I love to ride Black." She sipped her tea. "I don't even mind the pigs except when I'm chasing the little porkers in the middle of a thunderstorm."

Vera displayed a grin and asked Meggie to tell her all about the night it stormed. She laughed at the appropriate times and admitted it must have been a challenge to be alone on the farm in the middle of a tornado warning. "Someday, dear, you'll think back and smile at the fond memory."

Meggie shrugged. "You might be right, but at this moment I would rather file it in the back of my mind and not think about it."

"That is understandable. Fred had tales to tell, too. I remember when he bought the property." Vera ran her finger around the rim of her cup and gazed through the small window above the breakroom table. "He had so many plans for the farm."

"Who did he buy the property from?"

Vera pressed her lips together and one eye squinted. "An older man owned it, but I can't recall his name. Anyway, when he died Fred bought the property from the man's son. I don't remember if he tore the entire house down, but I do know he built a good portion of the farmhouse standing today."

The conversation turned to the abandoned well. Meggie explained how she discovered the well and what she had done to cover it up. She didn't mention the part about cold air rising up from its depths and enveloping her. Vera would only worry if she knew that part of the story.

"Did Fred have any animals?" Meggie asked.

"Oh, my, yes. I never visited the farm but he would talk about them when he came into the shop. He raved about his horse. I believe he called him Cloud, a big white stallion."

Meggie helped herself to a second cookie. "Tell Nettie her turtles are very good." She munched on the cookie. "Did you know Fred well?"

"I'd call him an acquaintance." Vera pushed her eye glasses further up on the bridge of her nose. "Before his wife passed away, he'd come into the shop and we'd converse. He loved to surprise his wife with a gift and never missed an occasion to do so."

Vera's face held a soft expression. "I enjoyed our talks, but at that time there were no policies on smoking in public places. Fred Jackson loved his cigars."

Meggie's face grew pale. A knot formed in the pit of her stomach. She set her cup down on the table and shifted in her chair.

Vera tilted her head and her brows drew together. "You don't look well, dear. Are you feeling all right? Perhaps you'd like another cup of tea?"

"No, thank you." Meggie looked at her watch. "I really should finish that last bit of inventory and then I must be going. I have a couple errands to run before I return to the farm."

Vera slid her chair back and started to clear the table. Meggie objected and promised to take care of the clean-up. When Vera turned to go, Meggie asked, "Do you still have that book on ghosts you checked out at the library?"

Vera's posture straightened and she turned around. "Why, I certainly do." She walked to the desk, retrieved the book and handed it to Meggie. "It's not due back until later this month. That should give you plenty of time to read it." She pointed her finger at the book. "I do hope you haven't been having problems with that sort of annoyance at the farm."

"Nothing I can't handle." Meggie's smile wavered and she looked at her watch. "I better hustle if I'm going to finish that inventory before we close."

Time passed quickly and before Meggie realized how late it was, she heard Vera announce they would be closing shop. She entered the last item on the inventory list and set the documents into the file cabinet. In the breakroom she snatched a turtle cookie from the cookie jar and strode to the front of the shop.

The window shade behind the till had been pulled down. Eldon stood near the door with the deposit bag in his hand, his head bent low while Vera whispered in his ear. They looked up when Meggie entered the room.

"I hope I'm not interrupting anything." Meggie cocked her head and looked from Vera to Eldon. "What are you two cooking up?"

"We weren't going to say anything, but I told Eldon if I don't tell someone I'll burst." Vera giggled like a schoolgirl. "Meggie, you're the first person to hear the news. Eldon and I are getting married!"

Meggie's eyes lit up. "Congratulations!" She threw her arms around Vera then circled her arms around to include Eldon as well.

She leaned back and looked him in the eye. "All I have to say is . . . what took you so long?"

LATER THAT EVENING, MEGGIE sat up in bed, fluffed a pillow and set it behind her. She opened the book Vera lent her and turned to the table of contents. Her eyes scanned the list of chapter titles until she came to one titled "Characteristics of Ghosts." She noted the page number, turned to it and began to read.

According to the author, ghosts could appear in different forms. They might appear as orbs or they could be translucent masses. Other times they might take on the shape of a person. She reread the last sentence. Her eyes darted around the room and she drew her feet close to her body.

One paragraph explained about the phenomenon of orbs and related stories from people who captured them on photographs. In many cases orbs appeared as translucent or solid circles. Some believed they were proof of guardian angels while others believed they proved the presence of ghosts.

The next part of the chapter referred to witnesses. Some witnesses stated they experienced a drop in temperature when a ghost presented itself. More than one described smells dispersing in the air around them. A chill traveled her spine. She closed the book and dropped it to the floor.

When Meggie reached toward the bedside lamp to switch it off, the light began to flicker then went out. She drew her hand back and wondered if the cord had worked its way out of the socket. She folded the covers back and lowered her feet to the floor. Her hands followed the lamp cord to the wall socket where she found nothing amiss.

Molly had not mentioned any electrical problems to her. Meggie felt her way down the bed toward the overhead light switch. Before she reached the switch, the bathroom light came on. Something squeaked from inside that room. Vanity door? Hair lifted on the nape of her neck. She crept closer and peeked into the bathroom.

The room stood empty but the noticeable scent of Old Spice cologne infused the air. Meggie's eyes swept over the room. Her legs felt weak. The ceiling light flickered, then the room went black.

Meggie turned and stumbled back toward the bed. She jumped in, slid under the covers and pulled them up to her chin. Her heart thumped. A creak near the bedroom window. Another at the end of the bed. The bedside light flashed on.

Meggie lifted her head slowly and peeked over the covers. Footsteps shuffled and the bedroom door quietly closed.

CHAPTER 7

I N THE MIDDLE OF THE WEEK, Meggie drove into town determined to search out information. Too many unexplainable events had happened since she arrived at the farm. Too many events to ignore.

Pine Lake Library was housed in one of the earlier brick buildings in Pine Lake. It sat across the street and two blocks down from the Legion Club. Meggie pulled the door open and quietly closed it behind her.

Maud Nelson, the librarian, sat behind a desk near the checkout counter and tucked a gray hair into the bun at the back of her head. She stood up, smoothed her dress down and carried a short stack of books through a door directly behind the counter.

Meggie waited at the checkout area and glanced around the library. The building appeared deserted except for a young woman who slumped in a chair near the back of the room and paged through a magazine.

When Maud returned from the storeroom she moved aside a stack of DVDs on the counter in front of her and clasped her hands together. "Hello, Meggie. How are you?"

"I'm fine. Who wouldn't be on a nice day like today?" Meggie shifted her weight from one foot to the other and settled her purse over her shoulder.

"How can I help you?" Maud's right eye twitched. "I wouldn't think you had much time to read these days." She leaned over the counter. "Francis Johnson stopped in the other day and told me you were housesitting a hobby farm near Bluff."

"News travels fast, doesn't it?" Meggie knew Maud Nelson liked to keep the small town grapevine swinging. "Actually, I'm looking

39

for information on a person who disappeared several years ago from the Bluff area. It might be a long shot, but I know in the past this library stored old newspapers in the back room. The library in Bluff is closed for renovation so I couldn't check there."

"Do you have a date in mind?"

Meggie shook her head. "I really don't know the exact date but I believe he went missing about eight or nine years ago."

Maud glanced around the room, leaned over the counter for a second time and whispered, "You don't mean Fred Jackson? He went missing about the same time as Amelia Schmidt."

"Yes. Fred Jackson." Meggie blinked. "Who's Amelia Schmidt?"

Maud smirked and kept her voice low. "Some believe Mr. Jackson and Mrs. Schmidt ran off together." She straightened up and waved her hand in dismissal. "But you know how some people around here like to talk."

Meggie rubbed the back of her neck. "I most certainly do."

Anyway," Maud's heavy-lidded eye squinted, and she pursed her lips. "I believe Fred and Amelia went missing about the same time as the Foxville bank robbery." She tapped her forefinger on the counter. "Wait right here."

She turned around and walked back into the storeroom. A few minutes later she returned and set several newspapers in front of Meggie. "You should be able to find something in one of these. I always make it a point to save newsprint that reports important events in the area."

Meggie carried the newspapers to a corner table, pulled out a chair and sat down. She looked at her watch. There was little time before she needed to head back to the farm. She slid her chair up to the table and unfolded the first newspaper. The front page headline shouted, "Bank Robbery in Foxville."

The headline jogged her memory. She recalled hearing about the robbery at one time but the details of the crime escaped her. Before reading the article about the bank robbery, she scanned the newspaper for a missing persons report on Fred Jackson, but found none. She looked the paper over a second time but still had no luck in finding any mention of Fred Jackson.

The second newspaper, dated a few days later, reported no missing persons but new information turned up on the Foxville bank robbery. A witness had stated she had seen a silver motorcycle leave the scene of the crime, but no arrests had been made.

Meggie frowned, set the newspaper aside and picked up the last newspaper. Her eyes moved up one column and down another on the first page in search of any news about Fred, but she came up short.

On the second page she hit pay dirt. A short paragraph at the bottom of the first column reported Fred Jackson missing. The authorities asked anyone with knowledge of his whereabouts to please come forward. She found no mention of Amelia Schmidt.

Meggie leaned back in her chair and drummed her fingers on the table top. Why would Fred Jackson just up and leave his house? Who was Amelia Schmidt and why did people think they ran off together? While someone had reported him missing, why had no one reported her missing?

If she guessed right, there must have been gossip about Fred and Amelia before they disappeared. Small-town busybodies had a way of distorting and twisting facts. The rumors about the two of them undoubtedly fueled the gossipmongers. Before anyone could stifle the falsehoods, they were accused of having an affair.

Meggie was all too aware how small town gossips worked. They had no boundaries and delighted in spreading lies to neighboring towns via friends, relatives, and even strangers.

When Fred and Amelia disappeared around the same time, it cemented the belief in those narrow minds that the two were having an affair and had run off together. On the other hand, the rumors could be true. They may have proved the gossipmongers right and done just that.

Meggie leaned her head against the palm of her hand and closed her eyes. There were too many unanswered questions. She knew her insatiable curiosity had landed her in trouble more than once. But if her questions were to be answered, she needed to find out more about Amelia. She folded the newspaper, set it on top of the others and slid her chair back.

At the check-out counter she handed the newspapers to Maud. She thanked her and turned to go but halted when the librarian asked in a low voice, "Did you find what you were looking for?"

Meggie lifted her shoulders. "The newspapers were helpful but I still have unanswered questions."

Maud crooked her finger and motioned Meggie closer. "It's possible one of Fred's hired hands bumped Fred off."

"Are you thinking of anyone in particular?"

Maud nodded. "I don't know the man's name, but he walked with a limp. He came into the library with Fred one day. I didn't trust him from the get-go. He gave me the heebie-jeebies."

Meggie didn't know what to make of Maud's information. "Did you tell anyone about your suspicions?"

"I mentioned it to one of the deputies at the Law Enforcement Center. He told me a man couldn't be arrested for giving someone the heebie-jeebies."

Meggie concealed a giggle and glanced at her watch. "I better hurry. The animals are waiting for me."

CHAPTER 8

THE NEXT DAY A HUMMINGBIRD beat its wings and hovered over the front porch feeder. It sucked at the red nectar then flitted away. Meggie closed her eyes against the sun. Her breathing slowed and a calmness descended over her.

Her mind wandered to the Caribbean Sea, a cruise ship, and the vacation she always dreamed of but had never taken. She could feel the ship's deck beneath her feet, the wind in her hair and the sun on her face.

The phone rang and her daydream crashed. She pushed herself out of the rocking chair and rushed into the house to answer it. "I would never get Walter aboard a cruise ship anyway," she mumbled to herself.

Meggie snatched the handset from the cradle and found herself pleasantly surprised to hear Shirley on the other end of the line. Her friend had not been home the day she called to invite her to lunch. She never returned her call and didn't answer the several voice messages left for her.

More than once the thought crossed Meggie's mind that perhaps Shirley planned to keep a low profile while she housesat at the farm. She understood her friend's feelings and why she wanted nothing to do with housesitting. Shirley had become involved in more than one of Meggie's unpleasant housesitting adventures.

Meggie carried the phone into the living room and sat down in the armchair. She listened as Shirley apologized for not returning her calls. Her friend faulted Bill, her husband, for not telling her about the calls. She went on to say that Bill erased the messages before she could listen to them.

The conversation turned to the hobby farm. Meggie thought about confiding in her friend about the bizarre incidents that had taken place since she arrived, but thought better of it.

After several minutes of catch up, Shirley invited Meggie to ladies night at Billy's on the Bay. She offered to pick her up at the farm and act as designated driver. "I'll spend the night at the farm if you'll invite me, but you need to promise you won't involve me in anything life-threatening."

Meggie laughed and promised she wouldn't intentionally put her friend in harm's way. "You'll be safer spending the night here than driving back to Pine Lake so late. It sounds like fun." She leaned her head back on the chair and rubbed her eyes. "I think I'm ready for a break."

Plans were made for girls' night out, and later that afternoon Shirley's bright red Taurus careened down the driveway. It made a U-turn in front of the house and abruptly came to a standstill, dust clouded around the car. Shirley honked the horn a couple times and shouted from inside the car. "Get a move on or we'll miss two for one."

Meggie pulled the front door closed, hurried across the porch and down the steps. She slid into the passenger seat and buckled her seatbelt. "Give me a break. I accomplished quite a lot since you called. The eggs are collected, washed and in the refrigerator. The chickens are ready to roost, and the pigs are securely latched in their sleeping quarters."

Shirley narrowed her eyes. "Their sleeping quarters?"

"Molly grew tired of chasing pigs so she devised a pig-proof pen. She bought a large folding dog kennel at a garage sale and set it around the outside of their hut. At night a padlock is slipped on the kennel door."

A puzzled look crossed Shirley's face. "Why the padlock?"

"The pigs learned how to lift the latch on the kennel gate with their snout. You wouldn't believe how smart those porkers are. Molly told me they chewed through the fence one time. They even tried to dig and root their way to freedom."

Meggie recounted the night of the storm and how she forgot to slip the padlock on the kennel gate. The pigs took advantage of her forgetfulness and broke free. As Meggie's story unfolded and she came to the part about falling in the rain-soaked muck, Shirley started to giggle.

"What's so funny?"

"Remember when I said Walter should put you on a short leash? Maybe a harness would be better."

Meggie laughed in spite of herself and visualized the scene, down on all fours in the muck and slime with a harness strapped on. "You're too funny. By the way, I left the horses in the pasture. You promised we'd be home early."

"Don't worry. I see no reason why we won't be home in time to bring the horses in for the night. We'll have time to do whatever it is you do before putting them to bed." Shirley's eyes gleamed. "Tonight will be my first lesson in horse care. I have a lot to learn about them and farm life in general."

After driving a short distance, Shirley glanced at Meggie. "By the way, Walter dropped off the hornet spray at my house on his way to work. You have hornets on the farm?"

"It's for self-defense." Before Shirley could make a snide remark Meggie continued, "They say it works better than pepper spray."

Shirley rolled her eyes. "I might believe some of the daft ideas you come up with if I knew who 'they' were."

When Meggie and Shirley arrived at Billy's on the Bay, the parking lot overflowed. Shirley circled the area a couple of times then spotted a car backing out of a parking space close to the front of the restaurant.

Another driver faced Shirley and waited for the same space. As soon as the car backed out and drove off, Shirley pulled in ahead of him.

"Shirley," Meggie scolded. "You just stole this space from that driver."

"First come, first served." Shirley turned the car off and glanced sideways at Meggie. "Don't worry, he'll find another place to park." She tilted the rearview mirror, applied a bright shade of pink lipstick and smacked her lips. "By the looks of this parking lot you would think no other establishment offered two for one. Either that or there's some thirsty ladies around." She grabbed her purse and turned toward her friend. "Let's hit it."

Once inside the restaurant it became apparent that Billy's on the Bay had become quite popular. Meggie looked around the eating establishment and suggested they sit in the bar area. "I had no idea it would be this busy. With all these guests we'll be lucky to make it home before dark."

"Let's hope the service in the bar area will be faster than in the dining room." Shirley started for a table and quipped over her shoulder, "We'll be closer to the bar. I hope their Shirley Temples are good."

LATER WHEN THEY LEFT THE RESTAURANT, the sun had almost disappeared behind the horizon. "I'm really sorry, Meggie. Who would have guessed it would take us this long for a couple drinks and dinner?"

"Don't worry about it. Molly told me she's been working with the horses to come when called. If we're lucky, they'll be close to the barn by the time we reach the farm. It won't take long to tuck them in."

"Afterward you'll fix me a cold gin and tonic and we'll spend a quiet evening on the farm, right?"

CHAPTER 9

W HEN THEY ARRIVED at their destination and turned into the
driveway, the car's headlights split the black wall in front
of them. No welcome lights shone from inside or outside
the house.

The women navigated in the dark and slowly made their way
to the front door. Meggie slipped the house key into the lock, reached
in and flipped the light on in the entryway.

"Where am I going to sleep?" Shirley asked and followed her
friend inside.

"You can have the small bedroom," Meggie moved up the
staircase ahead of Shirley. "There's no bathroom upstairs so you'll have
to use the one off the master bedroom on the first floor. I know it's
not very convenient." Meggie stopped and turned around. "If you want
to be closer to the bathroom, I could bunk on the couch in the family
room and you could sleep in the master bedroom."

"Don't worry about me. The upstairs bedroom will suit me just
fine. You know, I've never stayed on a farm before." She paused. "Actually, I've never had the desire to, and I certainly don't have it on my
bucket list like some people I know. But I am looking forward to it."

Shirley puffed her way to the landing, threw a hand to her chest
and paused to catch her breath. "I think I ate too many of Billy's French
Fries." She continued into the bedroom and set her bag down by the bed.
She strode toward the window. "It looks like we might have a little natural light after all. I see the moon peeking out from behind some clouds."

"Moonlight would be nice. We better hurry. I'll feel better once
the horses are rounded up." Meggie glanced down at the sandals on
Shirley's feet. "You better change into your walking shoes. You did remember to bring them, didn't you?"

47

Shirley screwed up her face. "Of course I did. Give me a little credit, will you?"

A short while later the women walked along the fence line near the house, armed with flashlights. Few trees stood in this pasture which made it easy to spot the horses during the daytime. Not so at night.

Meggie halted, swept the flashlight from side to side and called the horses by name. She waited a short time and called again. When the horses didn't respond both women headed toward the back pasture near the barn.

When they reached the back fence, Meggie's hopes were dashed. Black and Beauty were nowhere to be seen. She cupped her mouth and called the horses by name, but after several attempts it became obvious they weren't in any hurry to come in.

"You better give them another holler." Shirley slapped a mosquito on her face and another on her arm. "These blasted mosquitos are on the attack."

"Let's go look for the horses. I don't think I should leave them out there." Meggie turned her flashlight on Shirley.

"Look for them?" Shirley threw her arm out and pointed. "Out there? In the dark?"

"You can wait for me in the house if you'd rather. I don't mind going alone." Meggie strode to the gate and opened it. "Coming or not?"

Shirley glanced back toward the house then aimed her flashlight in front of her and marched through the gate.

"Watch out for the meadow muffins," Meggie warned.

"Meadow muffins?" Shirley faltered. "Are they any relationship to cow pies?"

"Yup, they sure are. Cousins, I think."

The moon hung from a black-blue sky and spilled light across the pasture. Frogs croaked from the nearby swamp and in the distance a coyote howled. They hadn't gone far when Meggie nudged Shirley with her elbow and pointed. "There's a brook up ahead. Over there through the trees. We'll check it out when we go riding."

Meggie marveled at nature's night sounds. Did senses heighten when the sun went down? She started to voice her thoughts when she sensed a presence nearby.

She halted and swept the flashlight all around. Several yards to her right stood an impressive white horse. The animal turned its head toward her, tossed it in the air and galloped off.

"How did that horse get in this pasture? There must be a gate I don't know about or a broken fence."

"What horse? What are you talking about?"

"You're telling me you didn't see that white horse over there?" Meggie beamed the flashlight on the spot where the horse had been.

"No, I didn't see any horse. I didn't hear one, either." Shirley paused. "You must have imagined it. Let's get going."

"I didn't imagine anything. It stood right over there, looked at me and then galloped toward that hill up ahead." Meggie thought about Fred's white stallion and her stomach tingled. She desperately needed Shirley's reassurance, but her friend was adamant. She had not seen a white horse.

Meggie dropped the subject. She raised her hands to shout for Black and Beauty then lowered them. "Did you see that?"

"See what?" Shirley whined and stepped closer to Meggie.

Meggie pointed straight ahead. "A light flashed over there on the other side of that hill."

"No, I didn't see any light but I'm beginning to get the creeps." Shirley lowered her voice and whispered. "Let's go back home. The horses must want to spend the night in the pasture or they would've come back to the barn. It won't hurt them to sleep outside, will it? I mean horses should be okay doing that."

"I'm going to check out that light." Meggie quickened her step. "We're not far from the base of the hill."

"Listen, friend," Shirley hurried to catch up with her. "You promised a pleasant evening after two for one, but here we are trekking across a field in the dark."

Meggie shushed Shirley and lowered her voice. "It's not dark, we have our flashlights, and there's a moon. Don't you think it's odd someone would be out in the middle of a pasture at night flashing a light around?"

Shirley panted. "I think it's odd you and I are out in the middle of a pasture at night flashing our lights around. But then I remind my-self who I'm with and it all seems perfectly normal."

Meggie ignored Shirley's jibe and continued on her way until she reached the base of the hill. She extended an arm in front of her friend and whispered. "Listen. Do you hear that grating sound?"

"Yes, I hear it," Shirley's voice shook. "It sounds like someone's digging."

"I'm going to find out what's going on. Why don't you wait here for me?" She turned her flashlight off and handed it to Shirley. "Turn your flashlight off and don't make a sound. I don't want who-ever it is to know we're here."

Shirley began to object but Meggie held her finger to her lips and shook her head. "I won't be long," she whispered.

After a short distance, the ground gradually inclined. Meggie leaned forward, put one foot in front of the other and trekked upward. Part way up the knoll she heard footsteps and a clinking noise behind her. She looked back at a dark shape clamoring up the hill after her. She might have been scared, but Shirley's voice quelled that.

"You're not leaving me." Shirley took a deep breath. "If you think I'm hanging out down there by myself . . ."

"Come with me but we have to be quiet." Meggie reached for her flashlight. "Let's go." She crouched low, slunk up the hill for a few feet then dropped to all fours and crawled.

Near the hilltop she flattened herself on the ground. She pushed her feet against the rocky soil and inched her way up until the top of her head was level with the hilltop. Shirley slithered in beside her.

"Hey, Sarge." Shirley rested her head against the rocky soil and gulped air. "I did good, right?"

Meggie smiled and patted Shirley on the back. She slowly raised her head until she could see over the hill. Her eyes surveyed the surrounding area and settled on an imposing black figure several yards away near a copse of trees. A light shone on the ground beside him.

The brawny figure bent over and thrust a shovel into the ground. He straightened up, flung the shovel's contents on the ground beside him then plunged it further into the earth.

Meggie had seen enough. She tapped Shirley on the shoulder and pointed toward the farmhouse. In a whisper she directed her to start down the hill, but cautioned her to go slow. If they could reach the bottom of the hill without arousing suspicion they had it made.

Meggie drew in her stomach, pushed against the ground with her hands and squirmed backwards. After several feet she pushed herself to all fours and crawled backwards.

But when Shirley attempted to push herself up on all fours, her right foot slipped and dislodged several rocks. They clattered down the hill.

Meggie experienced a quick intake of breath. She grabbed her friend's arm and lay still. The digging stopped. A hush fell over the hillside. Seconds later light flashed above them, moved from one side of the hill to the other.

"You should have brought your hornet spray!" Shirley hissed.

As if manna from heaven, the digging resumed. Meggie let out a long breath and raised her eyes heavenward. She rolled over onto a grassier area, crawled backward until she could stand without being seen and hurried down the slope.

When Shirley reached the base of the hill she bent over, hands on her knees. "I need to catch my breath," she panted.

Meggie gave her friend time to recuperate then grabbed her by the arm and pulled her along. "Let's get out of here. We'll have to forget about the horses. They're on their own tonight."

When they finally stumbled up to the pasture gate near the barn, they were shocked to see Black and Beauty waiting for them.

Shirley groaned and threw up her hands. "You've got to be kidding me. All that and the horses were here all the time? My first lesson in horses and what did I learn? How to survive a brush with Indiana Jones."

But Meggie couldn't have been happier to see Black and Beauty. At least she wouldn't spend the night worrying about them. On the other hand, she anticipated little sleep after this late night escapade.

THE NEXT DAY AFTER SHIRLEY had gone home, Meggie glanced through the kitchen window. If she hurried she might be able to catch the sunset. She wiped the counter, tidied up the kitchen and put on her summer loungewear.

From the refrigerator she pulled out the pitcher of iced tea she made earlier and poured a tall glass. She carried it to the front porch and set it down on the little table next to the rocking chair.

But before she sat down, she scooped up a cupful of sunflower seeds from a metal container and poured them into the bird feeder. That done she collapsed in the rocking chair, threw her feet on the footstool, and sat back to enjoy the sun's spectacle.

Nature didn't disappoint. The sun glowed on its descent below the horizon and left in its wake a palette of vibrant colors splashed across the sky, hues in reddish-orange and shades of violet. But the awesomeness of nature could not dispel the unease that spread over Meggie's being.

She never believed in ghosts. They were made up, Halloween characters. Even now after all the unusual goings-on she couldn't bring herself to admit they existed. She didn't want to believe this farm was haunted, but how could she explain away the cigar and cologne smells? How could she explain the chill in the air near the old well when the thermometer hovered around eighty degrees? The white horse and all the other incidents?

Why did she hesitate to tell anyone about the strange occurrences that had taken place? Was she afraid people would think she believed in the supernatural? Her mind whirled with unanswered questions. Uncertainties she didn't want to think about.

The evening wore on. Her mind calmed, and she reposed deep in thought. The glass of iced tea sat untouched and grew warm on the table next to her. She closed her eyes and dozed.

When she awoke the night had grown close with no breeze to relieve the stuffiness. The vibrant colors displayed across the sky had faded. The moon hung high in the sky and shadows appeared before her. Far off a dog barked.

Meggie stopped rocking and pushed herself up from the chair. As she turned toward the front door something flashed in the corner of her eye. A movement among the weeping willow branches. Her senses alert, she studied the towering tree but nothing stirred. Only still boughs draped amid the shadows.

A shaky laugh escaped her and she chided herself for being spooked. She turned away from the graceful tree but a force tugged at her and she turned back. The willow branches parted and a white horse appeared in a haze. The magnificent animal raised its front legs in the air, stood on its hind legs then dropped down and raced past the porch towards the backyard.

Meggie stood transfixed for several seconds unable to believe what had just happened. Adrenaline shot through her. She ran across the porch and down the steps. When she reached the backyard her eyes searched for the white horse but it had vanished.

She backed up, whirled around and ran into the house. A slight shiver trickled down her spine when she recalled Vera's words—"I believe he called him Cloud, a big white stallion."

A short time later no lights burned in the little farmhouse. Meggie lay in bed, her head spinning. She pulled the sheet up to her chin and concentrated on happy thoughts. But soon a dark thought wormed its way in, crawled through her mind and whispered in her ear, "The horse made no sound."

CHAPTER 10

A FEW DAYS LATER, Meggie hummed to herself at the kitchen table. She stuffed a letter into an envelope, addressed it and placed a stamp in the corner, then leaned it against the sugar bowl. Eve Moore Davenport, the only child of Walter and Meggie, would throw up her hands and shake her head when she picked up the letter.

A Seattle attorney, Eve's mission for the past few years had been to bring Meggie into the world of technology by harping on the same old, same old. "Mother, you really must learn to Skype. Open a Facebook account. Buy a Smart phone."

Just a month ago Meggie sent Eve a letter. Her daughter responded by phone. "But Mother, who writes letters anymore?" To which Meggie replied, "I do and I will continue to write letters for as long as I please. Society does not dictate to Meggie Moore."

She whistled on her way into the mini-pantry next to the kitchen and came out with a bottle of rum. She set a tall glass on the counter, added ice and measured one shot of alcohol into the glass. After adding more than enough tonic water and a squeeze of lime she stirred it, picked up the mosquito repellant and flipped off the kitchen light.

In the fading light Meggie followed the path to the gazebo, determined to enjoy the balmy evening. She sat down in the wicker chair and set her rum and tonic on the small table next to her. A warm breeze blew through the open structure. The moving air might be a mosquito deterrent. But to be on the safe side she applied repellant cream liberally.

Twilight came and turned the sky a pinkish hue. Tall jack pines near the front fence line grew dark against the evening sky. The moon rose and spilled its light over the backyard. Meggie leaned back to gaze at the multitude of stars dotting the heavens. An earthy smell and the sweet scent of petunias wafted through the air.

She closed her eyes, slave to a warm summer evening. Close by frogs croaked and crickets chirped. Soothed by the magical ambience, Meggie nodded off and fell into a deep sleep. She woke much later to a world swathed in darkness and the recognizable smell of cigar smoke. Her posture stiffened. She looked around to see if someone lurked nearby, but a black curtain had descended around her.

Her heartbeat raced. Alone and vulnerable, she no longer felt at ease. Her hands searched the darkness to find her way out of the gazebo. At the entrance she stepped out and placed one foot in front of the other. She struggled to maintain her balance.

When Meggie neared the house an odd feeling came over her and she raised her eyes. Low light shone down from the attic window. A black shape twisted, lengthened then vanished.

For a moment she couldn't move, unable to believe what she had witnessed. Then reality hit her. She spun around, retraced her steps to the gazebo and stumbled inside. Her eyes shot back towards the lighted window, but the house now stood shrouded in black. Hairs on her arm lifted.

Someone lurked in the attic. She needed to call for help but she had left her phone on the kitchen table. No way would she go into the house to get it. The closest neighbor lived across the road. If she tried to run over there, the intruder might see her.

The farm down the road. She could make a run for it through the horse pasture. She probably wouldn't be seen from the house, but how would she find her way in the dark? A voice inside her head cautioned her to do something, anything. She rose from her crouch. A door slammed on the other side of the house. She flinched, hunkered back down. Footfalls thumped. Seconds later an engine whined then roared to life.

By the time she pulled herself together, a banana shaped moon had appeared. It shed a faint glow around her. She stooped low, moved alongside the house and peeked around the corner. Two red taillights bounced up and down the driveway, then disappeared out of sight.

She scrambled onto the porch and ran to the front door. Inside the house she turned the lock and flipped the light switch. Her hands trembled as she punched 911.

Sometime later a sheriff's car pulled into the yard, lights flashing. The driver's door swung open and a tall well-built deputy climbed out of the car. A second deputy exited the passenger side of the vehicle.

The driver led the way to the front door where Meggie waited. "Meggie Moore? I'm Deputy Timothy Jarvis." He turned toward the second officer. "This is Deputy Ryan Flynn." Following introductions Deputy Flynn turned on a flashlight and jumped off the porch. He headed around the side of the house.

Deputy Jarvis followed Meggie into the kitchen where she explained to him exactly what had taken place earlier in the evening. She related how she made herself a drink, carried it to the gazebo and sat there until after dark. Tired from a long day, she dozed off and didn't wake until much later.

Because she had forgotten to take her flashlight with her and didn't think to turn the yard light on, it was dark when she started for the house. Before she reached the back door she noticed a light and shaded movement in the attic.

Deputy Jarvis jotted down notes for several minutes, then lifted his head. His eyes swept over the room past the kitchen window, the back door and finally over the half-empty bottle of rum on the kitchen counter. He rubbed his nose with his index finger and jotted down additional notes.

When the officer finished recording the evening's events, he tilted his hat back on his head and focused his eyes on Meggie. "Which way to the attic?"

She motioned the officer to follow her upstairs, led him through the first bedroom and into the second bedroom. She switched the overhead light on and pointed to a trapdoor in the ceiling.

"It's an old trapdoor, not attached to anything. I'm not sure why they call it a trapdoor. It's more like a hole in the attic floor covered with a piece of wood."

Deputy Jarvis raised his head upward, his attention fixated on the trapdoor located directly above him. He locked his eyes on the rectangular indentation for several seconds and scratched his cheek. He looked at Meggie. "Is there another way into the attic?"

Meggie shrugged. "I don't know of any. Like I mentioned before, I'm just the housesitter. The owner mentioned this trapdoor in passing the day she walked me through the farmhouse."

Heavy footsteps pounded the stairs. Deputy Flynn appeared in the bedroom. "No one outside and I didn't find anything unusual."

Deputy Jarvis nodded and jotted down a couple notes. He looked at Meggie. "We'll need to clear the attic, make sure no one is still up there." He thumbed his ear. "Any idea where we could find a ladder?"

Later that night after the house and property had been thoroughly searched and no intruder found on the premises, the deputies left.

Walter arrived soon after even though Meggie maintained she didn't need anyone to spend the night with her. He insisted on it and that was that. When he encouraged her to give up the housesitting job and ask Molly to come home, she insisted on seeing the job through and that was that.

BRIGHT AND EARLY the next morning Meggie introduced Walter to the farm animals. She gave him a play by play account of her duties and expressed her disappointment when he announced he wouldn't be able to help with chores.

"I already made plans with Bill to go fishing on the river. I don't want to back out of them. But I could drive out afterward and spend the night with you."

"That won't be necessary." Meggie looked at her wrist watch. "You better hurry if you don't want to miss the catch of the day."

On their way out to the truck he turned to her with a pained expression on his face. "Under different circumstances, I'd like to stay and help with the chores."

Different circumstances? Meggie didn't buy it. She knew her husband well enough to know there'd never be different circumstances. He couldn't wait to get home, hook the boat trailer up to his truck and head for the river. Farm animal chores were not on his bucket list.

Meggie thanked him for driving out to the farm and kissed him goodbye. "I know you're disappointed you can't stay longer. The next time I'll give you a heads up so you don't make any commitments. How does that sound?" Her eyes danced.

"Uh, that might work. I guess I better get a move on." Walter fidgeted with his car keys. "Are we still on for tomorrow?"

Meggie nodded and agreed to meet him at the boat landing as planned. She waited until his truck was out of sight then headed to the backyard to finish her chores. On the way she noticed the grass needed to be mowed. And the queen would have to mow it.

By the time Meggie finished cutting the grass she was tired, hot and thirsty. She parked the mower in the garage and pushed the button on the automatic garage door. Looking forward to a quiet afternoon of relaxation, she crossed the front yard. On her way she noticed the flower bed around the birdbath had overgrown with weeds. The unwanted plants had taken over the little garden space.

Ugh, not today. A gentle breeze blew the pretty pansy blooms. They nodded their heads as if to say, "Rescue us." She bent over and snipped off several flowers and promised herself to clean out the bed later that day.

In the bathroom she gazed at her sun-kissed reflection, ran cold water over a washcloth and held it to her face. The cool moisture soothed her burning skin. After rubbing aloe vera gel on her face and arms, she went into the kitchen to find a vase for the flowers.

A tiny glass vase hid in the corner of the cupboard. She filled it with water. As she dropped the pansies into the water a loud knock sounded on the front door. She set the vase down, walked through the living room and peeked out the window. Her brows furrowed. No vehicle sat in the yard. The rapping grew louder. She tucked her hair behind her ears and opened the door.

Donna Jones stood on the porch, nose pressed to the screen. The older woman's eyes lit up and her mouth spread into a smile when she spotted Meggie. "Hello there, neighbor," she said in a sing-song voice.

She held up a plate of red, white and blue cookies. "Since you couldn't join us for our Fourth of July celebration, I told myself I must save you some of my delicious sugar cookies all dressed up in patriotic colors."

The cookies weren't the only ones dressed up in patriotic colors. Donna's ruffled apron looked like a flag.

"Thanks. How thoughtful of you." Meggie invited her in and carried the cookies into the kitchen.

"I said to myself on the way over here, 'Self, I bet she'll make a pot of coffee to go with these cookies'." She giggled a bit and sat down. Her eyes roamed around the room. "There's nothing like a nice cup of coffee to go with a special cookie even on a hot day. Don't you agree?"

Meggie didn't agree but she smiled and filled the coffee maker with water.

Donna scooted her chair closer to the kitchen window and stretched her neck over the pile of mail that lay nearby. She inched her hand toward the stack of envelopes and used the tip of her index finger to slide the top piece of mail gently off the pile.

Meggie kept an eye on her nosey neighbor while she changed the filter on the coffee machine and added fresh coffee grounds. By the time she pushed the start button, Donna had worked her way down to the third envelope.

"The coffee'll be ready in a jiffy. Do you take cream or sugar?"

Startled, Donna pulled her finger away from the pile of mail and left the envelopes kittywampus. She brushed the gray hair away from her face and blinked rapidly. After composing herself she said, "A little of both please."

"Would you like some vanilla ice cream with your cookies?" Meggie set the vase of pansies in the center of the table. Laughter bubbled up inside her. She wanted to reach in front of Donna and straighten the mail but remembered her manners and behaved herself.

"I love ice cream." Donna paused and seemed to gather her words before speaking. "Did you have problems over here last night? I could have sworn a car with flashing lights drove up your driveway."

Molly had been right again. Donna was a nosy neighbor and right to the point. Meggie now understood the cookies had been a ruse to pump her for information about the previous night's activities. But she wouldn't fall prey to Donna Jones and divulged little.

As it turned out, her nosy neighbor was also a walking history book and the best search engine around. She seemed to know all about the neighbors, their children and how long they resided in her neck of the woods. Anything Meggie asked her she had an answer for.

Since Donna seemed more than willing to talk, Meggie thought it the perfect opportunity to ask a few questions. But her guest's facade changed when she broached the subject of Fred Jackson and Amelia Schmidt. She squirmed in her chair and seemed reluctant to answer any questions about them.

Meggie tried a different approach. "How well did you know Fred?" She waited on pins and needles to see if the woman would be forthcoming.

"Of course we knew Fred as a neighbor. We lived right across the road from him, you know." She scraped a dried crumb off the table with her thumb. "We worried about him. The way he hired men off the street to help him on the farm. Kind of risky, if you ask me."

"I suppose you knew Herman Schmidt, too?"

Donna closed up at that point and gave little information. But during the conversation she did mention her grandson and Herman's grandson had been friends at one time.

"Of course, my grandson didn't have much to do with Darrell for quite some time before the bank robbery." Donna sucked her cheeks in and crossed her legs.

"Bank robbery? You mean the one in Foxville?" Meggie prodded.

"Why, yes, the bank robbery in Foxville. You do know Darrell Schmidt went to prison for his part in the robbery, don't you? He was the getaway driver." She ran her finger on the side of her lip. "I do believe he received a shorter sentence due to his turning state's evidence. They may already have released him."

"I imagine Darrell's arrest created a lot of excitement in the neighborhood."

"I won't forget that day. It was my birthday and I had a chocolate cake in the oven. Fred's boar got loose. It took off down the driveway and ended up in our garden. By the time Fred and I corralled that pig I was fit to be tied. And my chocolate cake burned to a crisp."

A short while later Donna stood up and thanked Meggie for her hospitality. On her way out the door she glanced back at Meggie and smiled. "Did you know you have weeds in the pansy bed?"

CHAPTER 11

THE NEXT MORNING AFTER CHORES, Meggie slipped on jean shorts and a tank top. To be on the safe side she stuffed a light jacket into her backpack along with her fishing license, sun block, and cell phone.

Before leaving the house she locked the back door and closed the kitchen curtains to keep the sun out. She grabbed a couple apples from the refrigerator and several containers of bottled water. At the front door she tapped her bottom lip, mentally checked to make sure she hadn't forgotten anything, then closed the door after her.

Minutes later the Bug bumped along the dirt road. The morning sun scaled the tall pines and hung high in the sky. Meggie rolled the driver's window down and inhaled a deep breath of fresh air. She adjusted the car radio, slumped back in the driver's seat and kept time to the music.

The Bug rolled through Bluff and onto Highway 52 where it picked up speed. Within a short time a sign came into view on the side of the road and gave directions to the north side of Spirit Lake. Meggie slowed the Bug and turned right onto a paved road that eventually turned into gravel.

The gravel road wound around the lake past several houses. As she traveled on, the area became more isolated. There were fewer residences but more trees and foliage. She followed the bend in the road and soon came upon a sign that marked the public landing. Turning right she followed a narrow dirt road through the trees and into a clearing.

There were two vehicles in the parking lot but neither one belonged to Walter. Her eyebrows narrowed. She checked the time and found to her surprise that she had arrived early.

Meggie whistled a tune while parking the Bug then stepped out of the car into the bright sunlight. She strolled to the water and sat down on the bench near the landing. Shielding her eyes from the sun, she gazed out at the gentle rise and fall of the sun-tipped swells. She closed her eyes and inhaled the freshwater smell. The waves lapped against the shore.

A moment later she squeezed sun block on her arms, spread it over them and onto her legs. When finished she stood up and walked closer to the water. There she studied the latest information regarding noxious weeds posted in a secured enclosure by the Department of Natural Resources. She glanced at her watch, concerned. It wasn't like Walter to be late.

A low rumble caught her attention. She expected to see Walter's truck pull into the parking area any second. The low rumble grew into a roar and an oversized black pickup truck propelled itself through the trees. The driver swung to the right and backed the boat trailer toward the landing.

When the driver spotted Meggie, he braked the vehicle. The beefy man squeezed out from behind the driver's wheel and slammed the truck door. "You lost, Meggie? Or just running away?" Detective Lars "Bulldog" Peterson stood near the truck and removed his sunglasses. His grin spread ear to ear.

"Always the jokester, Bulldog." Meggie clenched her jaw and strolled toward him. "You haven't changed much since high school." She sized up the detective's shiny truck, smiled up at him and crossed her arms. "Actually, I'm waiting for Walter. We're taking our brand new pontoon out on the lake today."

"Nice day for it." Bulldog arched his back and puffed his chest out. He scanned the shimmering blue water. "I took the day off and plan to catch me a few sunnies. Probably not much else biting in this heat."

Following a moment of silence, he turned back to Meggie. A slow smile grew on his beefy face. "I hear you're housesitting a hobby farm now." He leaned against the side of the truck and twirled his sunglasses.

"As a matter of fact, I am." She narrowed her eyes. This man had been a thorn in her side for years and never missed a chance to needle her. "You must be referring to my 911 call? I'm sure by this time you've seen the deputy's report."

"Now Meggie, don't get your dander up." Bulldog teased. "We've known each other a long time, so friend to friend?"

Meggie nodded, and he continued.

"It's a professional worry for me when you take on those housesitting jobs. A personal one, too." He scratched his neck. "Seems like trouble has a way of ferreting you out."

"Let's call a truce then." Meggie struggled to find the right words. A flush crept across her cheeks. "I know I saw an intruder in the attic whether anyone believes me or not. I really did."

Bulldog pushed himself away from the truck. "From my understanding, the deputies did a search of the house and property." He hesitated, peered down at Meggie and dropped his voice. "They even pried open the trapdoor. They could tell it hadn't been used in a while."

Meggie's hands curled. "I know what I saw. I don't imagine things."

"Let's sit a minute." Bulldog pointed to the bench and hung his sunglasses from the neck of his shirt.

Meggie lowered herself onto the bench.

Bulldog plopped down beside her, leaned over and rested his forearms on his thighs. He didn't say anything right away, just stared out across the water.

After a few seconds he sat up straight and swiveled his head toward her. "I don't want you to take this the wrong way, okay? And what's said at Spirit Lake stays at Spirit Lake." He grinned at his own joke.

Meggie's palms began to sweat and she wiped them on her jean shorts. "Go ahead."

Bulldog cleared his throat. "I read the deputy's report yesterday. They didn't find anything or anybody that would prove there had been a break-in. No forced entry."

"I didn't have the doors locked."

"Nothing had been disturbed or seemed out of place in the house—downstairs, upstairs or in the attic."

"I saw an intruder in the attic," Meggie sputtered.

Bulldog turned and faced Meggie head-on. "The deputy did observe something and wrote it down in the report. After I read about his observation I got to wondering."

"I knew they would discover something. Tell me." Meggie's eyes took on a bright look. She clasped her hands and sat breathless.

"Well," Bulldog paused, "He observed a bottle of rum on the kitchen counter that appeared to be half-empty."

Meggie's jaw dropped and her eyebrows rose. She jumped off the bench, her muscles quivered. "Are you trying to imply . . ."

Bulldog slapped his knee and rose to his feet. "There you go again. You're way too sensitive for your own good. I'm not trying to imply anything. I'm only telling you what the deputy observed and wrote in the report."

He craned his neck at the rumble of a vehicle and the clank of a boat trailer, took a step backward and raised his hand. "I have to unload my boat and get my truck and trailer out of the way. You have a good day. Don't let the sun burn you."

Sun burn me? No sunburn compared to the pain you inflicted. And you didn't even give me a chance to tell you about Indiana Jones. But what's the point? You already think I have no gumballs left in my machine.

Bulldog backed the boat trailer into the water and braked. He jumped out of his truck and climbed into the boat, plunked down behind the wheel and started the engine. The boat puttered toward the dock. A look of surprise crossed his face when he saw Meggie waiting on the dock to secure his boat so he could park his vehicle.

Minutes later his fancy fishing boat skimmed over Spirit Lake, churned blue water into frothy foam and spread a wake to each side. The boat circled Camper's Island and disappeared from view. Were fish attracted to fancy fishing boats?

A SHORT WHILE LATER, the pontoon bobbed up and down near one of the smaller islands on Spirit Lake. Meggie sat under the canopy, tossed her fishing line in the water and called to Walter. "And that's not all. Do you know what Bulldog insinuated?"

At the front of the pontoon Walter reeled in his line. He checked to make sure the fish hadn't stolen his bait and cast the line back into the water. "No. I don't know what Detective Peterson insinuated." He tossed a dead minnow into the water and watched a gull swoop down after it.

Meggie flared her nostrils. "He had the audacity to insinuate I was drunk the night I called 911 and reported an intruder. Can you believe it?"

Walter pulled the bill of his cap low on his forehead. He turned away from the sun and scrutinized Meggie. "Why would he think that? Were you tipping the rum bottle again?"

Meggie clicked her tongue. "You're just trying to push my buttons, but it won't work. You know as well as I do that I don't drink much. I had one weak drink. The nerve of that man. He made me sound like I'm some kind of lush."

Walter sat with his back to Meggie, cast his line into the lake and didn't say a word. He didn't have to. She knew what he was thinking. He had the annoying habit of laughing so hard his shoulders shook.

CHAPTER 12

THE FOLLOWING MORNING, Meggie washed the last breakfast dish, set it on the drain board and wiped her hands on the kitchen towel. She gazed out the window above the sink and drummed her fingers on the counter. Her blood boiled every time she thought of Bulldog and his insinuations about her drinking. She took a deep breath and walked out of the kitchen.

Meggie hurried down the porch steps and crossed the yard in the direction of the garage. She lifted the short step ladder off the hooks, set it across the wheel barrow and wheeled it back to the house.

In the upstairs bedroom, she spread the ladder's legs until they clicked into place and slid the ladder over until it stood directly under the trapdoor that led into the attic. With latches secured, she placed her hands on the sides of the ladder, stepped on the first rung and began to climb.

Near the top of the ladder she stretched her arm toward the trapdoor. When she couldn't reach it she climbed to the next rung, placed her right hand against the ceiling and pushed up. The ladder wobbled under her and she steadied herself. The second time she shoved up and pushed the trapdoor over. The opening yawned above her.

Her head moved slowly up through the hole in the floor until she could see into the attic. The entire room stood empty. The air smelled musty. Muted sunlight shone through one small window on the attic wall to her left. Dust particles floated in the light stream, zig-zagged on the way down and drifted out of sight.

Meggie held onto either side of the gap, planted her foot on the next ladder rung and climbed into the attic. She sat down on the edge of the opening and removed the flashlight from her pocket.

The light flashed around the empty room. It didn't take a rocket scientist to figure out why the deputy's search had ended almost before it began. He could view the entire attic without stepping foot in it.

The window facing the road appeared to be broken. Upon closer inspection she found several pieces of glass on the floor beneath it. Was the storm to blame? She made a mental note to board up the broken window and let Molly know about it.

She turned away from the window and began to make her way around the attic when she noticed shoe prints in the dusty floor. Her pulse raced. She knelt down to get a closer look and waved the flashlight over the floor in front of her. There were several small clumps of dirt strewn about. The shoe prints seemed to go in different directions but ultimately ended up by the attic window that faced the backyard.

The deputies had pried the trapdoor open, which could mean only one thing. If the intruder didn't use the trapdoor to get into the attic, he entered another way. She retraced her footprints to the trapdoor to verify the prints left by the intruder did not start there.

Eager to find a second way into the attic, Meggie began to circle the area. Unfinished walls sprouted worn insulation and several pieces of dusty lumber lay on the floor nearby. Midway in her search the light flashed over a black area. She pointed the light into the dark cavity and gasped.

In the semi-darkness she could see a narrow set of wooden stairs. She stuck her foot out and tapped the first stair. It felt solid enough so she set her foot down and edged her way into the close area.

She felt somewhat constricted but descended the stairs one by one. The glow from the flashlight bounced in front of her and onto a second set of footprints. She gripped the flashlight and carefully stepped around the second set of footmarks.

After several stairs she came to a dead end and could go no further. A thin layer of light shone at the bottom of the wall to her right. She pushed against the wall but nothing happened.

She turned to ascend the staircase but her foot slipped off the bottom stair tread. She fell to her knees. In an attempt to right herself she noticed the stair tread shifted. Curious she aimed the flashlight, wiggled the tread and lifted up.

Her breath hitched. Several yellowed envelopes lay inside the hollow stair. She fingered the envelopes—all addressed to Fred Jackson in what appeared to be feminine handwriting. Her fingers lingered on the top one.

She weighed the pros and cons about removing mail that didn't belong to her, but determined that under the extenuating circumstances it would be all right. She gathered the letters together and carried them up the stairs.

When Meggie reached the trapdoor she tossed the letters through the opening. She stepped onto the first rung of the ladder and continued downward until her feet rested on the solid bedroom floor.

She collected the letters, carried them into the first bedroom and set them on the bed while she conducted her investigation. If her guess was right, the door leading to the hidden staircase would be in this bedroom. She focused her eyes on the wall near the bedroom door. They came to light on a small narrow bookcase.

Meggie removed the books from the bookcase and placed them on the floor. She tried to slide the bookcase out of the way, but it held fast. She stood back, studied the timeworn paneling and pushed a second time. Upon closer inspection she realized the bookcase had been fastened to the wall.

She grasped the side of the bookcase and pulled. The wall section grated and swung open. Natural light from the bedroom shone across the hidden staircase. Her lips parted in a satisfied smile and she pushed the door back into place.

Meggie walked to the window and gazed outside. She pinched and tugged at the bottom of her lip. If Molly knew about the secret staircase wouldn't she have mentioned it? Maybe not, but it didn't matter. What mattered was the fact that someone out there knew about it. The question was who.

Downstairs she carried the yellowed envelopes into the kitchen and laid them on the table. At the sink she filled a glass with water, carried it back to the table and sat down. She sipped the water and slipped on her readers.

Her hand hovered over the stack of letters for several seconds. She snatched her hand back. She didn't feel good about snooping and had always been taught it was wrong to read other people's mail. She rubbed her wrist with her thumb.

Why did she feel compelled to read the letters if she wasn't meant to? She pulled her chair closer to the table and gathered the envelopes together. They were all addressed the same way—To Fred.

Meggie took a deep breath, opened the first envelope and slipped out the letter. She set it down on the table and laid the envelope next to it. After all the envelopes were opened and the letters unfolded, she organized the letters by dates.

Her hand trembled as she picked up the first piece of paper. She read it and slipped it back inside the envelope. She went on to the next letter and the next until the last letter had been read and placed inside its envelope.

The letters told a story. Not the whole story, but a story. Meggie closed her eyes in an attempt to see into the past. Amelia in an abusive relationship, void of love. And Fred. All alone since the death of his wife. Amelia and Fred find each other later in life and fall in love.

Meggie opened her eyes. She glanced down at the letters and pondered. How did their fairytale end?

CHAPTER 13

EGGIE LIKED MONDAYS and looked forward to what the week
had in store for her. She stuffed the paper bills deep in one
pocket, a plastic shopping bag in the other and set a sun visor
on top of her head. She pulled the front door closed behind her and started
down the driveway. If she hurried she could get a walk in, stop by the neighbor's vegetable stand and return to the farm all before Shirley arrived.

At home she preferred to walk early in the morning when the
neighborhood hadn't fully awakened. She loved to hear the birds chirp,
feel the cool air on her face and smell the freshness of nature.

Since coming to the farm she never walked in the morning or
any other time of the day. Once she finished taking care of the animals, the house and the yard, she had no ambition left to walk.

This morning Meggie lacked her usual amount of energy. She
had trouble falling asleep the night before, unable to put thoughts of
the intruder, letters, and ghosts to rest. Her mind had churned with
visions. When she finally fell asleep the visions turned to dreams.

At the end of the driveway she turned right and quickened her
pace. If she remembered correctly, the vegetable stand was located about
a half mile down the road. She reminded herself to buy a small amount
of vegetables since they would weigh her down on the walk home.

A tractor rumbled towards her from the opposite direction. As
the farm vehicle neared, the roar grew louder and dust mushroomed
over the road. The driver raised his hand in greeting.

Meggie moved to the side of the road and fanned her face as
the old farm machinery rolled by. It looked like the same tractor she
had seen parked in Donna's yard on occasion. The driver could be her
grandson. Donna mentioned he helped his father with farm work on
his days off. She wondered if he still considered Darrell a friend.

LATER THAT MORNING she heard a car drive into the yard. She set the filled water bottles on the table and went to answer the door. Before she could open it, Shirley barged through. Meggie took one look at her and started to laugh.

"What's so funny?" Shirley straightened her back and threw her hand on her hip.

"I'm sorry, but it's your hat." Meggie wiped a tear from her eye.

Shirley twisted her sombrero and narrowed her eyes. "You told me to wear a hat, and this sombrero happens to be the only one I could find." Her face fell. "It brings back memories of the trip Bill and I took to Mexico. Don't make fun."

Meggie apologized and assured her the hat would do just fine. She took a quick look at her friend's footware and signaled a thumb's up sign. "Good choice on the hiking boots. It's important to have a sturdy pair of boots or shoes for the stirrups. By the way, did you remember the information for Audrey's surprise party?"

"I have it all right here." Shirley tapped the side of her shoulder bag. "I assume I'm staying in the upstairs suite tonight?" She started toward the staircase and remarked over her shoulder. "I'm glad you agreed to work with me on plans for Audrey's birthday party. She's going to be so surprised."

A few minutes later Shirley sat at the kitchen table and waited for Meggie. When her friend walked out of the bedroom sporting a dark-brown cowboy hat and matching leather boots, she stood and checked out her friend's ensemble. "Did you ever talk Walter into buying a pair of cowboy boots?"

Meggie shook her head.

Shirley followed her out the back door. "I thought as much. Obviously, he hasn't changed his mind about riding the range with you. But you never know, he might have a change of heart."

Meggie strode towards the barn and tried to ignore her friend's badgering. She had grown accustomed to it after all these years, but some days she just wasn't in the mood.

Shirley hurried to keep pace with her. "I mean, get real, Meggie. After that last housesitting adventure of yours who can blame him? I'm surprised he lets you out of the house. Face it, you almost got us—"

Meggie stopped and crossed her arms. She noticed the sombrero had taken a dive over her friend's eyes and reached out to push it up. "How many times am I going to hear about the last adventure? And the adventure before that? And before that?" She lifted her eyebrows, pressed her lips together and resumed her stride. "I don't need to be reminded all the time about our past exploits."

"You don't have to be so testy," Shirley called after her. "I was just saying. Bulldog hit the nail on the head when he said you were sensitive."

Meggie swung the barn door open and motioned her friend to go ahead of her into the dim interior. Once inside Shirley hung back and waited for Meggie to lead the way to the horse stalls.

"There sure aren't many windows in this humongous building." Shirley's eyes gave the barn a once over.

"You're right. I haven't figured out why, but there must be a reason for it. Four windows don't allow much natural light inside."

At the stall Meggie stroked Black's forehead then buried her face in his long neck and took a deep breath. "I love the smell of horses."

Shirley crossed her arms and sniffed. "I don't know about horse smells, but something reeks."

Shirley walked over to Beauty's stall and timidly reached for the mare's forehead. She rubbed it and eyed the barrel of the horse. "Let's hope those yoga stretches you talked me into doing work or I'll be walking around bowlegged."

Meggie laughed and waited for Shirley to familiarize herself with Beauty. She showed Shirley the proper way to curry comb and brush a horse. After they finished grooming the animals, Meggie bridled and saddled them the way Molly had instructed.

She checked each cinch a second time to make sure the saddles were tight enough and led the horses out of the barn. She handed the mare's reins to Shirley and tied Black to the fence.

A large wooden platform stood near the barn door. Meggie instructed Shirley to stand on top of it. "It'll be easier to get into the saddle. Just put your left foot in the stirrup and throw your right leg over the saddle."

After several tries, Shirley managed to mount the horse and wiggled into a comfortable position. A cheesy grin spread across her face. "So far so good. But what do you say we don't run the horses? I don't think I'm ready for that." She bent low, patted Beauty's neck and waited for Meggie to adjust the stirrups.

Meggie untied Black and opened the gate. She mounted the stallion and shook the reins. "Giddy up."

The leather saddle creaked as Meggie rocked slowly back and forth over the horse's hips. She glanced over her shoulder to check on her friend. Beauty hadn't moved away from the wooden platform.

"You need to give her more rein," Meggie called and lifted her arms to demonstrate.

Shirley took her advice and flicked the reins. Beauty pranced ahead and almost collided with Black.

"Whoa!" Shirley pulled back on the reins and brought the mare to a standstill. Her face lit up. "She obeyed me. I think I'm going to get the hang of horseback riding."

When Meggie suggested she ride Beauty up next to Black so the horses could walk side by side, Shirley jiggled the reins and urged her mount to move a little faster. Soon the two horses and their riders were traversing across the meadow.

CHAPTER 14

THE SUN BEAT DOWN from a big blue sky. An osprey glided over-head. The horses plodded on and left the meadow behind. From somewhere nearby the familiar cry of a killdeer rent the air. Meggie pointed the bird out, related how they made their nests on the ground and oftentimes faked a broken wing to distract preda-tors.

Soon open spaces gave way to wooded areas. Birch leaves rus-tled in the warm summer breeze and a woodsy pine perfume floated through the air.

The gurgling brook caught the rider's attention, and they coaxed their horses to the edge of its bank. A rabbit peered at them from the other side of the brook. The furry creature studied the horses and riders but soon lost interest. It hopped one way, then the other and finally sprang off into the woods.

They lingered until the horses grew restless. Insects attacked in droves. The stallion shook his head and swished his tail in an at-tempt to ward off the bloodsucking flies. Beauty became more agitated than Black. She flung her head up and down and lifted her back leg to brush off the pests.

"I think it's time to leave," Shirley remarked. "These deer flies must take steroids. They're big enough to pick me up and carry me away."

"I'm with you. What do you say we climb the hill?" Meggie laughed. "For old time's sake."

Shirley agreed to the suggestion and let Beauty follow Black's lead.

At the base of the hill Meggie leaned forward and grabbed the saddle horn. She moved in rhythm with the stallion. When they reached the crest, Meggie looked out across the property and listened to the clip clop of Beauty's hooves behind her. "We couldn't see much the other night. It's serene, isn't it?"

"I think we saw more than we expected or wanted to." Shirley lifted the brim of her sombrero. "You're right. It is serene."

"Make sure you don't hurry down the hill," Meggie advised when they were ready to leave. "The horses have to take it slow." She loosened the reins, leaned back in the saddle and urged Black on. The horse chose his footing carefully and soon reached the bottom of the hill.

Shirley rode up next to Meggie. She tipped the brim of her sombrero up and wiped the perspiration from her neck. "Where are we headed Kemosahbee?"

"I thought it might be fun to ride all the way to the back gate. It's a beautiful day to enjoy nature by horseback." She felt somewhat guilty for not disclosing the entire reason she wanted to ride to the back pasture line. But after her friend's earlier accusations and insinuations, she thought better of it. The less her friend knew the better off she would be.

"The back gate, huh? I get the feeling you're holding something back from me. Are we on a scouting expedition?"

Meggie laughed. "Why would you think that?"

"I know when you're hiding something up your sleeve. And you know I don't like to be kept in the dark. If you want to play detective just say so." She set her jaw and thrust out her chest. "It's rather rude to invite me on a horseback ride to enjoy nature, blah, blah, blah, when you have an ulterior motive."

"Hear me out," Meggie spoke up. "We both wanted to enjoy nature by horseback. You said as much to me the other day. I just thought that as long as we were out riding . . ."

Shirley rolled her eyes. "I knew it. I should have known better. Give it to me straight. What are you up to now?"

"It's a long story. What do you say we find a shady spot and take a rest? Then I'll fill you in." She pointed toward a large grove of trees. "How about over there?"

Once she reached the spot, Meggie dismounted Black under the shade of a poplar tree and wrapped the reins around its trunk. She removed her hat and wiped the sweat off her forehead then sat down on the log to wait for Shirley. She pushed the heel of her boot against the ground and thought about what she would tell her friend.

"You're going to dig yourself a big hole and fall into it if you're not careful." Shirley plunked down on the log beside her. "Oh, this feels good, doesn't it?" She nudged her friend. "All right, I'm listening."

Meggie related the conversation she had with Donna regarding Darrell Schmidt. "My neighbor thinks the system released him early. He could be out now."

"Is it safe to assume you've been doing a little investigative work regarding the bank robbers?"

"Only after I spoke with Donna."

Shirley frowned and pulled at her ear. "Didn't you mention that a Schmidt lived nearby?"

Meggie nodded and pointed to the right. "Herman Schmidt, his grandfather, lives in that direction. His property borders Riley's land. I put two and two together and came up with . . ."

"Darrell Schmidt buried the loot in the field. We caught him literally digging for gold or the next thing to it. Is that what you came up with?"

"I don't know for sure, but the possibility exists." Meggie stood up and put her hat on. Her eyes surveyed the area. "We saw him digging right around here, didn't we?"

She walked until she found a fresh mound of dirt, studied it for a minute and called out, "Here it is. I'm not sure what I expected to find, but there's nothing here." She strode back to the log and sat down. "There's something else I want to tell you."

Shirley twirled her sombrero and eyed Meggie.

"I told you about the hidden staircase."

"That's right. You promised to show it to me."

"Let me tell you about the letters I found the same day."

By the time Meggie finished her story, Shirley had stopped spinning her sombrero and her face held a blank look. "There's some truth to the rumors about Fred and Amelia. I wonder if her husband knew about their relationship?"

"That, I don't know. Should we saddle up and head in that direction?"

"You're not seriously thinking of checking out his grandfather's house, are you? That's trespassing."

Meggie shook her head. "No, let's just ride a little farther. I don't want to get involved in anything or snoop around. What's the point?"

"Right, Sherlock." Shirley groaned. "I've heard that one before."

Meggie led the way through an open area and into a grove of pine trees. She hadn't gone far when she heard a high-pitched bark. Seconds later a small light-colored puppy shot its head up through the tall grass and yelped again. It came bounding over.

Black fidgeted and backed away from the small creature. "I wonder if he's lost," Meggie called to Shirley and tried to restrain the horse. "He's a cute little fellow. Looks like a Labrador retriever."

"If he follows us when we turn around what are we going to do?" Shirley reined Beauty in close to Black.

"I've had second thoughts about going any farther. Let's start for the house and see if he follows us."

The puppy ran ahead of them. He stopped abruptly and chased his tail in a circle then spied a butterfly on a nearby clover. He ran to the clover, pawed the air and gave chase to the butterfly. Seconds later the puppy dashed past the riders.

"I suppose we better find out who he belongs to. It looks like we might make Mr. Schmidt's acquaintance after all."

They reversed directions and rode until they came to the back gate, found it open and crossed through. Meggie wrinkled her brow and looked back at the gate. "That isn't good. Black and Beauty could have gotten out."

"Why is there a gate here?"

"Molly told me that years ago the original owner of the property shared pasture space with the neighbor. I guess some of this fencing has been up for quite some time." Meggie wondered if Fred had never bothered to take the gate down for other reasons.

Pine needles crunched under the horses' hooves. They zigzagged in order to avoid the trees. When they had gone a short distance Meggie spotted an outbuilding. It looked in dire need of repair. She pointed it out to Shirley then turned in her saddle to make sure the puppy still followed.

They reached the Schmidt yard and several little puppies started to bark from a fenced-in area near the outbuilding. As she pondered how the little fugitive escaped the pen, he came scampering up to Black and wagged his tail.

Meggie climbed out of the saddle. She bundled the puppy in her arms and strode toward the back door to let Mr. Schmidt know the reason for their visit. She glanced around at her surroundings. The house needed a fresh coat of paint. A dilapidated screen lay on the ground under a broken window and several beer bottles lay strewn around an overflowing garbage can.

Meggie knocked on the back door, waited several seconds and knocked again. When she knocked for the third time it became obvious no one was at home. She turned to go when she caught a glimpse of someone inside the house.

The face wasn't distinguishable but the person had shoulder length hair. Meggie recalled her conversation with Donna. Perhaps

Darrell had been released from prison. An uneasy feeling settled over her.

"Let's get out of here," Shirley called from the saddle. There's no one around, and I feel like we're trespassing. Not to mention my rear end is getting sore."

"Just let me take care of this little fellow." Meggie carried the puppy to the dog pen. She set him inside and shook her finger at him. "You be a good little puppy now and don't follow us."

She noticed the latch hung loose on the pen. Lucky the other puppies didn't get out. She looked around for something to brace the door. A shovel lay beside the dog pen. She grabbed the handle and leaned it against the gate.

Meggie mounted Black. As she rode away from the house, she had the uncanny feeling a pair of eyes followed her.

BACK AT THE FARMHOUSE, Meggie handed Shirley a glass of lemonade and a plate of Double Stuf Oreos, then led the way to the front porch. She set her drink and a plate of ham sandwiches down on the table between the two rocking chairs.

Shirley carefully lowered herself into one of the chairs. After a long drink of lemonade, she helped herself to a ham sandwich and glanced at Meggie. "Are you worried about the person you glimpsed at Herman Schmidt's house?"

Meggie shook her head.

"You're pensive. That indicates there's something you're not telling me."

"Pensive?" Meggie toyed with her sandwich "That's a new one. Whatever makes you think I'm pensive?"

"Friend, I've known you for a long time." Shirley raised her eyebrows. "You're afraid to spill your guts about something. You can't fool this old girl."

"Why would I be afraid to tell you anything?" Meggie laughed and held Shirley's gaze.

"I can think of several reasons." Shirley tapped the arm of her rocking chair. "Reason number one is your aversion to the words I told you so." She leaned over, picked up an Oreo and broke it open. "Did you know that Oreos have become one of the best-selling cookies in the United States since they were invented in 1912?" She leaned back in the rocker and licked the frosting off the wafer. "I'm waiting, friend."

"You'll only gloat if I tell you."

"I won't gloat." Shirley leaned closer to Meggie. "At least I'll try not to."

Meggie wiped her mouth with a napkin and took a drink of lemonade. She set the glass down and picked up a cookie, debating how much she should tell her friend. "There have been some strange happenings since I . . ."

"I knew it." Shirley slapped her knee. "But you wouldn't listen to me. I warned you."

"You're gloating," Meggie warned with a penetrating stare.

"I'm sorry. Tell me. I promise not to interrupt." She clamped her lips together.

By the time Meggie finished her story, the color had drained from Shirley's face, and she had stopped rocking. "Then it is true? This place is haunted?" Shirley held her hand up. "I know I tried to talk you out of housesitting because Molly believed the house was haunted," she lowered her eyes and then raised them, "but I didn't really believe it myself."

"I didn't believe it either," Meggie's voice rose. "But how do I explain the smell of cigars and men's cologne?" She twisted her hands. "And I haven't told you everything."

Shirley scooted to the edge of the chair. "After Old Spice and cigar smoke, I can't wait to hear the rest of the story." She gestured with her hand for Meggie to continue.

"It happened one evening after I watched the sun set." Meggie glanced toward the weeping willow tree and took a deep breath. "I don't know how long afterward, but the moon had risen. The night was close. No breeze at all. That's why I thought it odd when the branches on the weeping willow tree stirred."

Meggie gripped the chair's arm and continued. "And before I knew what was happening, the branches parted and a big white horse walked out surrounded by a cloudy haze. The horse stood on its hind legs and pawed at the air, then dropped down on all fours and ran off."

"A white horse in a cloudy haze? Like the white horse you saw the night we played army?" Shirley bent forward. "It must belong to someone around here. The haze could have been the moon playing tricks on you."

"I wish it were as simple as that." Meggie's knee bounced up and down. "No one in the neighborhood owns a white horse. I checked."

"I'm not following. If Molly and Michael have no white horse and the neighbors have no white horse, where did it come from?"

Meggie hesitated. "Vera told me Fred Jackson owned a big white stallion named Cloud."

"Oh, my gosh." Shirley's eyes bulged. "Are we talking horse ghost?"

"Look at the evidence, Watson."

CHAPTER 15

T"O BE HONEST WITH YOU," Shirley said, rolling her shoulders and stretching at the kitchen table. "I thought I might find you this morning in front of a boiling cauldron reciting 'Double, double! Toil and trouble!'"

"'Fire burn and cauldron bubble!'" Meggie laughed. "That's witches, not ghosts. I may have a wrinkle or two, but so far no warts on my nose. And I don't wear a pointy hat."

Shirley chewed a bite of bagel and washed it down with a swallow of prune juice. "You're right. Ghosts and witches are not the same thing, but like it or not something strange is going on here. After what you disclosed yesterday, I could hardly sleep."

Meggie nodded. "Odd smells, white horses, no hoofbeats."

"And to top it off," Shirley threw up her hands, "we belly crawl to the top of a hill in the horse pasture and find Indiana Jones digging like his life depended on it. Then someone or something invades the attic!"

"You're right. Something strange is going on." Meggie pushed her plate away and crossed her arms. "I don't know if the supernatural events have anything to do with the treasure hunter or the intruder, but I have an idea how we might solve one of the mysteries."

Shirley stroked her neck. "We, as in you and me, solve a mystery? Been there, done that." She laughed from the side of her mouth but her eyes brightened. "What did you have in mind?"

LATER THAT MORNING when the farm chores were done, the women rested on the back patio. "We better get busy if we're going to carry out my plan," Meggie said. "We'll need a thick rope, and I know just where to find one."

The barn door rattled to the side. Meggie lifted the lantern off the wall and headed toward the far side of the barn past the horse stalls. Light shone over the corner of the building and settled on a thick rope hanging from the back wall.

Meggie stood on her tiptoes, grabbed hold of the rope and slung it over her shoulder. "This should work," she said and started for the barn door.

"What's the rope for?" Shirley questioned her. "You need to tell me what we're going to do. My life won't be in any danger, will it?"

"You won't be in any danger. Trust me." Meggie handed the lantern to Shirley while she slid the barn door back in place.

"I've heard those words before," Shirley mumbled to herself and followed her friend back toward the house.

"Here we are." Meggie tossed the rope on the ground. She kicked aside the excess birch debris left from the day Walter cut the tree up for firewood.

"Here we are." Shirley threw her hand on her hip and gazed around. "Where exactly are we? And now that we're here, what exactly are we going to do?"

Meggie knelt down and peered up at Shirley. "Can you help me move these bricks and plywood off this old well?"

"Old well?" Shirley set the lantern down and crossed her arms. "Before I expend another ounce of energy, I want you to cough it up and tell me what this is all about."

Meggie sat back on her haunches and looked up at her friend. A long sigh escaped her. "Long story short?"

Shirley gave her a curt nod. "Long story short."

"I think Fred Jackson is down there." She jabbed her finger over the well."

Shirley's chin dropped and her eyes opened wide. "Are you kidding me? The Fred Jackson who supposedly ran off with Amelia?" She lowered herself to Meggie's level. "Why on earth do you think he's down there? He's probably off playing footsie in some senior citizens home with his lady love."

"I discovered this abandoned well after the storm. When the birch tree toppled over, its roots jarred the concrete loose." Meggie nodded at the piece of concrete that lay close by. She lowered her voice and rushed her words. "After I uncovered the well, I peered in and something eerie happened."

Shirley quirked an eyebrow. "Something eerie?"

Meggie explained how a blast of cold air escaped from the well cavity, wrapped itself around her and dissipated.

"If you're right and Fred's down there, shouldn't we call someone, like maybe law enforcement?"

"Think about it." Meggie splayed her hands out. "Bulldog and probably half the department already think I drink too much. If I go in there and tell them there's a body at the bottom of an old well in the backyard where I'm housesitting, they'll think I'm a real nut job."

"I see your point. I have to admit I see their point, too." Shirley scratched her temple. "Correct me if I'm wrong, Sherlock, but are we going to use this rope to go well diving?"

Meggie shook her head. "Not we. I wouldn't ask you to do something that might put your life in danger. Your job will be easy, but first we need to remove these bricks and plywood."

Together they began to remove the bricks. When the last one had been taken off, they pulled the plywood away from the hole and set it off to the side.

Next Meggie took the end of the rope and wrapped it around one of the bricks. She leaned over the well and fed the rope through her hands until the block hit bottom. From her pocket she drew out a black permanent marker. She made a thick black line around the rope where it lay over the edge of the well. In her other pocket she carried a length of orange reflective tape she had scrounged from the trunk of her car. She brought it out and tied it around the black line.

She wiped the perspiration from her forehead and stood up. Hand over hand she pulled at the rope until the weight appeared. She set it on the ground and started for the back door. "Wait here. I'll be right back," she called over her shoulder.

The gardening bag sat inside the back door. She rummaged through it, found a pair of garden gloves and a hand trowel. In the bedroom she slipped on a pair of jeans and a sweatshirt, then removed the belt from her summer robe. She picked her car keys up from the kitchen table and hurried out the front door.

Inside the Bug she turned the key in the ignition and shifted the car into reverse. She backed around the side of the house and kept a close eye in the rearview mirror. The Bug skirted the clothesline, crossed over the path between the house and gazebo and stopped some distance from the well.

She killed the engine and stepped out of the car. With long strides she estimated the distance between the Bug's back bumper and the well. She spotted Shirley resting under the shade of a nearby oak tree and waved her over to the well.

After removing the block from the end of the rope she folded the rope end back and formed a small loop then tied a knot. She pulled it tight, tested it and pushed the other end of the rope through to form a larger loop. Close to the looped end she tied a couple of double knots.

"Here's how it'll work. I'm going to secure this end," she shook the unknotted end of rope in her hand and walked toward the car, "underneath the back bumper of the Bug." She lowered herself, stretched out on the ground and squirmed underneath the car.

Once the rope was secured she wriggled back out. She stood up and brushed herself off. "I'll use the loop at the other end of the rope like a swing and you'll lower me into the well."

"This is crazy! I didn't volunteer for assisted suicide duty." Color drained from Shirley's face.

"Don't worry, I'll be fine." Meggie threw her shoulders back. "The well isn't that deep. From what I can tell, it's partially filled with rocks and gravel. But it's a bit too deep for the step ladder. Besides, there's hardly room down there for me, let alone a ladder. Stand right there."

She walked to the gazebo, pulled a decorative garden stake out of the ground and carried it back to where Shirley waited.

Meggie's lips turned up at the corners. "You look as if you've lost your last friend. Really, it's going to be okay. I know a man who rescued his cat from a well. And he lived to tell about it."

Shirley looked doomed. "That doesn't make me feel any better. It only proves you're not the only screwball around."

Meggie tapped the stake against her leg. "We really don't have to do this if it makes you uncomfortable. I honestly didn't invite you to the farm to involve you in a caper. I thought you wanted to help me."

"Here comes the guilt trip." Shirley pressed her lips together and nodded. "All right, count me in. I'm a little curious about what happened to Fred, too."

"Great. When the back bumper lines up with this stake," Meggie pushed the stake into the ground next to the rope's orange reflective tape, "stop the car and turn it off. You'll be able to see the stake better if you hang your head out the window." Shirley groaned but Meggie continued giving her instructions. "By the time you've reached the stake, the orange reflective tape will be at the mouth of the well and I'll be at the bottom of it."

"Let's hope we pull this off or you'll be spending an awful lot of time with Fred." Shirley glanced at the well and shuddered.

"After you turn the car off, get out and walk over to the well to make sure I'm all right. It shouldn't take me long. When I'm finished just pull me up."

Shirley pinched the skin at her throat and met her friend's eyes. "I hope you find what you're looking for. You do know this stunt probably tops the list of absolutely crazy things you've ever done." She sighed. "And once again I've agreed to help with crazy."

Meggie wagged her finger back and forth. "Not crazy. Extreme perhaps. Maybe even daring, but not crazy. Are you ready?" Shirley nodded. "Good. Let's do it. Remember, back up real slow so I don't drop down too fast. We'll be done before you know it."

Shirley's shoulders slumped, and her feet shuffled on the way to the Bug. She glanced over her shoulder and warned, "Be careful."

Meggie tossed the hand trowel into the well and waited for the clunk on the bottom. She held the bathrobe belt in her hand and fed it through the lantern's handle. After she tied the ends together, she turned the lantern on and positioned the belt around her neck.

She slipped on the garden gloves, placed the looped end of the rope over her shoulders and underneath her bottom then sat down on the edge of the well. She flipped over on her stomach, grasped the double knot with both hands and slid off the side of the well where she dangled in the hollow space. "I'm ready," she yelled. "Take it slow."

The Bug slowly backed up. Meggie began to descend. She pushed her leg against the inside of the old well to center herself and bounced down a couple inches, then a foot. She gripped the rope and pulled slightly to lessen the strain on her bottom.

Sunlight faded as she sank lower into the well. The lantern jiggled against her chest and a soft light bounced off the well walls. To her surprise, the lining of the well appeared to be in good shape.

The rope scraped against the lip of the well. Dank air pressed in on her and an ache gripped the pit of her stomach. She clenched the rope tighter, drifted slightly and dropped several more inches.

Her back skimmed the brick-lined wall. She maneuvered herself away from it and looked into the void. The floor rose up to meet her. She stretched her leg until the tip of her shoe touched then rested on the rock-strewn bed.

A door slammed above her and seconds later Shirley hung her head over the side of the well and shouted, "Hey, are you all right down there?" Her voice echoed inside the well.

Meggie looked skyward and called, "I'm fine. Give me a few minutes." She squatted down into the small space, lifted the lantern over her shoulder and set it down beside her. The rock bed glowed under the lantern's light.

She shifted her weight and winced. Rough pebbles and little chunks of cement jabbed at her knees. She cleared the annoying stones away and resumed her position. Her eyes scanned the bed's surface. Several larger rocks had been tossed down the well onto smaller stones and gravel.

She leaned forward, hooked her fingers around one of the rocks and shoved it off to the side. She began moving more of the rocks. When the last big rock had been moved, she sat back on her haunches and studied the depressions in the floor.

She reached for the trowel and a woozy feeling washed over her. Her head began to spin. No way did she want to faint. Not here, not now. She hung her head and closed her eyes.

"Hey, what's going on down there? You feel all right? You're not moving," Shirley shouted.

In a few seconds the episode passed. Meggie lifted her head and shouted back, "I felt a little dizzy, that's all. I'm fine now." She picked up the trowel and scooped a pile of loose rocks and gravel up, then tossed them to the side and continued digging.

The sweatshirt that protected her skin on the descent into the well had now become uncomfortably warm. She lifted the sweatshirt's hem and shook it up and down to create a little air flow but it didn't help much. The well was short on room and short on oxygen. She wondered if she would last much longer.

Meggie shifted into high gear and thrust the trowel downward. The blade struck something. She dug around the area. A dark object protruded from the ground. She took hold of it and tugged, but it held fast. She cautiously cleared away more gravel. Her scalp prickled. She had uncovered what looked like the toe of a leather boot.

Carefully she continued her quest with the trowel then her gloved fingers. Finally, she found what she had been looking for. "Shirley," she screamed. "I found him!"

Shirley shouted back. "You found Fred?"

"I'm not positive it's Fred, but whoever it is, he's dead."

CHAPTER 16

LATER THAT AFTERNOON, Meggie handed Shirley a cola and suggested they sit on the back patio. She pulled the tab on her pop can, led the way outside and sat down. She said nothing, but her eyes were riveted on the well.

"What are you thinking about?" Shirley asked after a bit. "You're awfully quiet and that doesn't bode well."

"We need to drive to the Law Enforcement Center today." Meggie sipped her root beer. "I'm wondering how Bulldog will react when we break the news to him about Fred."

A fly buzzed around Shirley's soft drink. She brushed it away and chuckled. "You're worried Bulldog won't believe you, will insinuate you have an overactive imagination and, in his condescending way, will suggest you retire from housesitting." Shirley grinned and tilted her head. "Tell me I'm right."

"You might be." Meggie kept her eyes glued to the center of the backyard. "I do know how we might be able to prove to him that Fred is buried in the well."

Shirley frowned. "How do you propose to do that?"

Meggie stood up and looked down at Shirley. "We could take a picture of his ghost." Shirley opened her mouth to say something but Meggie held up her hand, instructed her to wait on the patio and rushed into the house. She returned with her digital camera.

Shirley shook her head. "Take a picture of Fred's ghost? You're serious, aren't you?"

Meggie sat down on the edge of the patio chair and adjusted her camera. "Remember when we spoke to that tour guide in Key West and he described orbs?"

Shirley smirked and nodded. "I remember. He said ghosts have been known to appear on photos as small white globules or orbs. Correct me if I'm wrong, but you were very skeptical and spent most of the night trying to explain away the phenomenon."

"You're right, but I've been doing some research on ghosts. Did you know they say you can actually talk to ghosts and ask them to show up in photos? Some orbs even have faces on them."

Shirley leaned forward. Her eyes squinted. "You mean to tell me you actually believe that?"

Meggie shrugged. "I'm not sure what I believe anymore. But what have we got to lose? We can take some pictures, see what happens and maybe convince Bulldog we know what we're talking about."

"I've accused you of having a screw loose before, but now I think it's fallen out and rolled away." Shirley shook her head. "But I suppose we have nothing to lose. What do we have to do?"

Meggie stood up and encouraged Shirley to follow her. She led the way toward the old well, stopped within several yards of it and put her finger to her lip.

"What's the matter?" Shirley spoke in a low voice and stood behind Meggie. "Are you going to talk to Fred's ghost?"

Meggie nodded and with a shaky voice addressed the ghost of Fred Jackson. "Hello, Fred. My name is Meggie Moore and this is Shirley Wright. We believe you're the one buried in the old well, but we need to prove this to the authorities." Meggie paused.

"This is giving me the willies." Shirley took a step backward and poked her friend. "Tell him to say cheese, snap the picture and let's get back to the house."

"Please pose for this picture." Meggie held up the camera and snapped the picture. She took several more then turned around and hurried back to the patio where Shirley waited for her.

Meggie's hands shook and her eyes grew wide as she examined each photograph. She looked at Shirley, handed her the camera and waited for her friend's reaction.

"LET ME GET THIS STRAIGHT." Detective Bulldog leaned forward in his chair at the Law Enforcement Center and zeroed in on Meggie. "You believe someone murdered Fred Jackson and threw him down the old well out at Riley's hobby farm. And you believe this because you felt his spirit ascend out of the well when you uncovered it the day after the storm. How am I doing so far?"

Meggie clenched her jaw and nodded, "That's right."

Bulldog pointed at Shirley. "So you tied a rope to the underside of Meggie's Volkswagen Bug and lowered your friend into the well so she could search for Fred's remains?"

Shirley slumped in her chair and stole a peek at Meggie then looked back at Bulldog. "Not exactly. Meggie tied the rope to the Bug."

Bulldog blew air through his mouth. He leaned back in his chair and looked up at the ceiling. After several seconds he stood up and walked to the front of the desk. He shoved aside a pile of papers, sat down on the corner and dangled his leg.

Meggie folded her arms and watched the detective's leg swing back and forth. She gave him a glassy stare. "I suppose you don't believe any of this?"

Bulldog took a deep breath. "I believe you're convinced someone murdered Fred. I believe you're convinced his spirit attached itself to you so you would search for his killer." He glanced at Shirley and then back at Meggie. "I believe you had your friend lower you into the well at the end of a rope."

He rubbed his right index finger against the back of his left hand and regarded Meggie. "I believe you found an old boot and some bones. Whether or not those bones belong to Fred is another story."

Meggie opened her mouth to speak, but Bulldog held up his hand. "I'm not saying they aren't Fred's bones. I'm just saying they might not be. Did it occur to you that some animal might have fallen down the well at some time?"

"There's one more thing." Meggie opened her purse and brought out the camera. "We have a picture of Fred's ghost."

Bulldog's mouth slackened. He gaped at Meggie. "Excuse me? You have a *photograph* of Fred's ghost?"

Meggie stood up and handed him the digital camera.

Bulldog slid off the desk and looked down at the picture. After several seconds he scratched his jaw and his eyes locked on Meggie. "Is this some kind of joke? I don't see a ghost or anything that might resemble one. All I see is a pigpen and a big old barn."

Meggie inched closer to Bulldog, leaned over the camera and tapped her finger against the tiny screen. Right there. It's called an orb."

"It doesn't have a face though," Shirley chimed in.

"Face?" Bulldog puffed out his cheeks and shook his head in disbelief. He handed the camera back to Meggie and rubbed his brow. "Tell you what. I'll see what I can do, but if we decide to check it out, we'll need to get in touch with the property owners."

Bulldog wrote down the information he needed and tossed the pencil on the desk. He opened the office door. "Ladies, we'll keep in touch." After he shook Shirley's hand he turned to Meggie, clasped her hand and held it for several seconds. "You're sure you don't have an overactive imagination?"

Meggie shook her head, peeked at Shirley from the corner of her eye and quirked an eyebrow.

Bulldog continued. "As one friend to another, I think you ought to retire from housesitting, Meggie. Stay home and take care of Walter. It's safer, and it'll keep you out of trouble."

The women left Bulldog's office and made their way down the aisle between several cubicles. In one cubicle a uniformed deputy sat at his desk, looked up as they passed by, then quickly looked away. A second deputy clicked on his keyboard and darted glances at them. Near the lobby door three deputies were deep in conversation, but fell silent when they saw Meggie and Shirley approach.

The women crossed the lobby. Meggie pushed against the glass door that led outside and held it open for Shirley. When they were several feet away from the building, Shirley glanced over her shoulder. "That went over like a lead balloon."

"At least he might have it checked out," Meggie shuddered. "Now I know what it feels like to walk the gauntlet. Did you notice how quiet it became when we walked by everyone?"

"Yeah, I'm sure they think you're loony." Shirley caught herself and quickly added, "I mean they think *we're* loony."

"Who cares what they think?" Meggie turned to Shirley. "I do have one question."

Shirley rolled her eyes. "I'm sure you do."

Meggie unlocked the driver's door and looked over the Bug's roof at Shirley. "If Fred rests at the bottom of the well, where is Amelia?"

CHAPTER 17

THE MURMUR OF CONVERSATION, loud laughter and clink of glasses slit the air inside the Legion Club. Walter held a tall glass under a beer tap and filled it to the top. He set it on the bar in front of a male patron.

Meggie looked away. She stirred her rum tonic and let her mind wander to the hobby farm. So much had happened since the day she drove out to Rileys' to housesit. She found it difficult to comprehend it all.

After Bulldog broke the news to Molly and Michael about possible human remains in the old well behind their house, Molly wanted to cut her vacation short and return home. But Meggie encouraged her to stay in North Dakota and enjoy the rest of her time with Michael. She promised Molly she would keep in touch if there were any new developments.

Walter leaned over and laid his hand on the bar in front of Meggie. "You're deep in thought. Something troubling you?"

Meggie started at his words. She swished her drink and contemplated a response. "Questions persist in my mind about the whole Fred and Amelia thing. I feel I should be doing something to find some answers. Now that the remains from the well have been positively identified as Fred's, I want to know what happened to Amelia."

"The authorities will investigate and find out who murdered Fred." Walter drew his hand off the bar and straightened up. "Whatever happened to Amelia doesn't concern you. Let it go and back off. Be grateful they've identified Fred's remains." Walter glanced at his watch. "Where are Bill and Shirley? They better get here if they don't want to miss the meat raffle."

A few minutes later, Shirley burst through the door and pressed her palm to her heart. "Thank heavens we're on time. I didn't think we'd make it." She gave Bill a curt nod.

"Don't blame me." Slighter and not much taller than Shirley, Bill defended himself. "You're the one who had to change clothes a hundred times."

Meggie grinned and slid off the bar stool. She led the way into the well-lit section of the Legion Club. Most of the tables were occupied with patrons hoping to win free steak or fish packages. She found an empty table near the pull-tab booth.

"Walter loves being in charge of the meat raffles. He thinks tonight will be very profitable for the Legion Club. Butcher's Meat Market donated the best-looking steaks." Meggie saw her husband approaching the table with a roll of raffle tickets. She dug in her purse and pulled out her wallet. "Here's hoping I win."

LATER THAT EVENING, Walter handed out the last package of steaks to the winning patron, picked up his drink and ambled over to Meggie's table. He sat down and asked her if she needed another drink, but she shook her head.

After congratulating Shirley on winning three steak packages, he turned to Bill and soon the men were deep in conversation. When Walter divulged that walleyes were biting on Rabbit Lake, plans were made for a fishing trip.

It grew quiet at the table, both couples lost in thought. Then Walter spoke up, "I talked with the commander of the Legion Club in Bluff. Fred was a member so they plan to hold a burial service for him."

Bill shook his head and piped in, "The authorities sure are keeping everything hush-hush. There's no doubt in my mind someone killed him. They suspect foul play, but so far no suspects have been identified."

"Sooner or later they'll catch the guilty party. Either that or it becomes a cold case, which would be a darn shame," Walter added.

The evening grew late. Only a few people remained in the club. Two couples occupied a table on the far side of the room. An elderly man nursed his beer at the table next to them. He seemed in no hurry to leave. Even the bar area boasted few hangers-on.

"Whoever killed Fred must be shaking in his boots." Shirley crossed her legs and swung her leg up and down." If it hadn't been for Sherlock and Watson, that poor man would still be lying at the bottom of an old well. I'd love to see the faces of all those gossipmongers who were so sure Fred and Amelia ran off together."

Meggie noticed the man sitting at the table next to them leaned in their direction. He must have been served one beer too many.

"As for the whereabouts of Amelia," Walter began, "I've already told Meggie to let go and back off." He glanced at his wife. "For once, I think she's going to take my advice."

As soon as Walter and Bill left the table to buy pull-tabs, Meggie set her drink down and turned to Shirley. "Here's what we're going to do . . ."

THE VOLKSWAGEN BUG CLATTERED across High Bridge from Duluth, Minnesota, to Superior, Wisconsin, under a gray sky. The St. Louis River churned beneath the bridge.

"Are you sure Amelia's sister lives in Superior?" Shirley glanced at the speedometer, then into the river. "You better slow down or we'll end up swimming with the fish."

Meggie kept her eyes on the road. "I've got the driving under control and no, I'm not sure Amelia's sister lives in Superior, but I'm keeping my fingers crossed."

"I hope you're right and this doesn't turn out to be another one of your featherbrained escapades. We both know it wouldn't be the first time." Shirley shook her head and let out a long breath. "By the way, who's Edith Knutson and how does she know Amelia's sister?"

"Edith and I met at Vera's shop. I worked with her at St. James church bazaar in Bluff." Meggie stopped at a red light. "Edith grew up with

Amelia in a small town in northern Minnesota. When they were young, they both relocated to the Bluff area. Evidently, they were fast friends until Amelia married her husband. After that, Edith rarely heard from her."

"I wonder what happened to their friendship? Do you think Amelia's husband put the kibosh on it?"

Meggie shrugged and drove on. "Edith suspected Herman didn't want his wife to have any friends, but Amelia never told her as much." Meggie flashed a quick look at Shirley. "I quizzed Edith about Amelia's disappearance to see if she knew anything. She told me rumors swirled around Bluff for years. Gossips said Amelia and Fred Jackson had a thing for each other."

Shirley's chin jutted. "So when they both went missing everyone assumed they ran off together. But now we know for sure Fred didn't run off with anyone. I wonder if Amelia is dead, too."

"I heard through the grapevine that some people think Amelia had something to do with Fred's death. But I don't believe it for a moment. You know how it goes. One rumor squelched and another one pops its ugly head up." Meggie glanced out the driver's window then back on the road. "I think it's only right, and Molly agrees with me, that we return Amelia's letters to her if she's alive."

"A shot in the dark," Shirley mumbled.

"According to Edith, Amelia's older sister married and moved to Superior. Edith didn't have an address for her, but she remembered Ruth lived near a park by Lake Superior. I did a Google search on all the parks near the lake."

"Just so we're on the same page. You think Amelia's sister lives in Superior but you don't know for sure. You think she lives near a park by a lake, but you can't be certain of that either." Shirley shook her head. "Like I said. A shot in the dark."

Meggie pulled off to the side of the street. "There's a park over there," she pointed to her left, "and that house right there is the only two-story home on the block." She looked at Shirley. "Are you coming with me or do you want to wait in the car?"

Shirley decided to wait in the car so Meggie made her way to the house alone. She pushed the doorbell and waited. Several seconds went by. When no one answered the door, she pushed the button a second time. After another short wait she turned toward the Bug and shrugged.

Behind her the door opened. A young woman with a child in her arms peeked out. When asked if Ruth Burnson lived at the address the woman shook her head. "If you give me a minute, I'll find her forwarding address." Minutes later she returned and handed Meggie directions to an assisted-living home.

Meggie slid into the front seat and buckled her seat belt. "She doesn't live here anymore, but the young woman believes she stills resides at Holy Angels, an assisted-living facility." Meggie pulled away from the curb and made a U-turn. She repeated the directions to Shirley, asked her to keep her eyes open for the street and turned left at the corner.

Minutes later she pulled up in front of Holy Angels. "Well, here goes. Let's keep our fingers crossed that Ruth still lives here and she can give us information about Amelia."

The two women crawled out of the Bug and walked up to the front door of the building. The glass door opened, and they stepped inside the small entryway. A directory on the wall to the right displayed initials, room numbers, and buzzers.

Meggie stepped closer and scanned the initials. At the very bottom of the list she spotted R.B. "I think we're in luck. Let's hope she's home." Meggie pushed the buzzer, heard a click and pulled on the lobby door.

Soft music played in the background. A number of armchairs were arranged around an oblong coffee table. Two loveseats sat opposite each other in front of a gas fireplace. A white-haired lady sat knitting at the end of one loveseat. She glanced toward the door and smiled at the two women.

Several small tables were positioned nearby. A food cart with carafes, mugs, and a covered food tray had been parked next to the tables. Two elderly men sat at the table closest to the cart and focused on a game of checkers.

Meggie looked around the area. "I don't see an information desk. Let's find room 119."

Shirley fell into step with Meggie and together they walked down the carpeted hallway. They passed several apartment doors decorated with wooden greeting plaques and other craft items of welcome.

"Here it is." Meggie stopped in front of room 119 and knocked on the door. She waited several seconds then put her ear to the door. Footsteps approached and the door knob turned.

A thin woman with salt-and-pepper hair adjusted her glasses and glanced up at Meggie. "May I help you?" she asked in a soft voice.

"My name is Meggie Moore, and this is my friend, Shirley Wright." She paused. "We're looking for Ruth Burnson."

"I'm sorry but she's out at the moment. I'm her sister. Maybe I can help you or let her know you stopped by."

"Amelia Schmidt?"

The woman nodded.

Meggie looked dazed. "We didn't expect to find you here. We thought you might be . . . I mean, we didn't know . . ."

Sometime later Amelia sat on a cream-colored sofa near a window in the sitting room, the package of letters beside her. She had expressed her sorrow about Fred's death and composed herself. "Thank you for telling me what happened to my Fred. I have always wondered." She took a deep breath and began to tell her story.

"Fred found my step-grandson's silver motorcycle in the brush near the pasture line between our two places. He remembered that a witness reported seeing a silver motorcycle speed away from the bank over in Foxville after the robbery. Fred got to thinking that Darrell might be involved in the crime and confronted him. He told Darrell to turn himself in or he would call the sheriff. Fred thought a lot of Darrell. And Darrell looked up to Fred."

"When did Fred tell you this?" Meggie asked.

"Right after he read the newspaper account about the silver motorcycle. It upset him to no end because he had taken Darrell under his wing time and time again."

"In what way?"

Amelia confided that her husband could be very abusive towards his grandson. "Fred knew how things were for Darrell at home so he gave him odd jobs now and then. That way Darrell could earn a bit of money. Fred was always helping someone. That's the kind of man he was."

Meggie glanced at Shirley and then back at Amelia. "Do you know if Darrell helped Fred close off the stairway to the attic?"

Amelia shook her head. "Fred closed off those stairs right after his wife died. She was quite young and pregnant with their first child. Fred came home one day and found her lying at the bottom of the staircase."

Meggie squeezed her eyes shut. "How awful."

"That's not to say Darrell didn't know about the stairway. He spent a lot of time at Fred's place." She paused. "I didn't know for years that Fred closed off the stairs to the attic. He could be very close mouthed. We didn't spend time together in his house."

Color rose in Amelia's cheeks. "Fred and I had become more than friends but we weren't lovers. I want you to know that. We both wanted more, but I had a husband, and Fred was a gentleman. He told me not to give up hope. We could work things out."

Her face tightened and her eyes appeared cold. "Folks gossiped about us being lovers for years. I'm sure you know how small towns are when it comes to fabricating stories." When the two women agreed with her, she continued on and seemed to choose her words carefully.

"Darrell acted real strange the night after Fred threatened him. It was late, and I had gone to bed but couldn't fall asleep. Darrell moved around in his bedroom for a time and then snuck out of the house."

Amelia wrung her hands. "I got out of bed and peeked through the window. I could see him in the moonlight. He walked into the shed and came out with a bag of something and a shovel."

Meggie leaned forward in her chair. "A shovel? Where did he go?"

"He headed for the woods. I knew my husband wouldn't be home until the bars closed so I followed Darrell. I kept my distance so he wouldn't hear me."

Meggie's stomach fluttered. "Did those woods connect with the back of Fred Jackson's land?"

Amelia nodded. She lowered her hand onto her lap, brushed her fingers across her dress and gazed out the window. "Yes, the woods started behind our house and ended near the pasture line. Fred and I loved to ride horses together. That's how our relationship began. Of course, Herman didn't know anything about it. At least I don't think he did. He was away from home a lot."

She turned away from the window. "Darrell went through the pasture gate and started digging on Fred's land. I couldn't see much, but I heard him. As soon as the digging stopped, I high-tailed it back to the house so he wouldn't catch me spying." She paused and caught her breath.

"A couple days later the cops came to the house, arrested Darrell, and took him away. I waited until my husband left for the bar that day. Then I took the shovel, walked back into the woods and dug up the money." Amelia's lips quivered and her hands shook. "I decided to talk to Fred. He would know what to do. But I couldn't leave the house for a day or two."

She started to cry and Meggie spoke up. "If this is too difficult to talk about . . ."

The older lady held up her hand. "Fred's truck was parked in the yard, so I knocked on the door. I waited a bit, and then let myself into the house. I called out for him, but he didn't answer me. Something didn't feel right. Fred didn't leave the door unlocked when he wasn't home."

"Wild thoughts went through my head. I suspected something happened to Fred. Darrell wouldn't harm him. I was sure of that. But my husband would. I thought about Fred's hired hands. Could one of them have done something to him? I was frightened. I didn't know what to do. I didn't want to go home. My husband was in such a foul mood after they arrested his grandson."

"Did Fred ever get in touch with the sheriff?"

"I never found out. I just wanted to get out of there and away before something happened to me. That's why I bought a one-way ticket to Superior and finally left that man. I tried to contact Fred when I arrived in Superior, but I couldn't reach him. He knew my sister's address but he never contacted me. A short while later I heard he went missing."

"Did your husband try to come after you?"

"No. I suppose he figured I ran away with Fred or maybe he suspected I had gone to live with my sister. Either way, he didn't care enough to come after me. Even if he did care, he had a stubborn streak. He always said he wouldn't chase a woman down. I haven't seen or heard from him since I left the farm." She hesitated and glanced out the window. "Although, there have been times I feel as if I'm being watched. It's hard to explain. I suppose it might be paranoia."

Amelia looked tired and Meggie wondered if they should take their leave when the apartment door opened. A woman who resembled Amelia walked in. She stopped mid-stride, looked from Meggie to Shirley with a probing gaze and set her purse on the table.

"We have guests, Ruth." Amelia smiled at her sister. "Come, meet Meggie and Shirley."

Ruth walked into the sitting area and sat down on the sofa next to Amelia. Ruth's face relaxed while Amelia explained to her the reason for their guests' visit.

A short while later Meggie looked at her watch. "I'm afraid we may have overstayed our welcome. It was nice meeting you both, but we really must start for home."

Amelia left the sofa, bent over and touched Meggie's arm. "Please, just a minute." She walked out of the room. Minutes later she came back carrying a dirty vinyl bag and held it in front of Meggie.

"Here's the money. Every last penny. I borrowed enough to buy a one-way ticket to Superior, but I paid that money back long ago." She placed the vinyl bag in Meggie's hand. "After I settled in Superior, I recalled that Fred planned to hire a man to help fill the old well. If only I had realized the importance of that information."

CHAPTER 18

MEGGIE STASHED THE BAG OF CASH in the trunk of the car, walked to the driver's door and slid into the front seat. She let out a deep breath and turned to Shirley. "What an amazing story."

"That poor woman. Her husband must have been a brute for her to run away from him like that. And all those years not knowing what happened to Fred." Shirley snapped her seat belt and looked back at the facility. "Talk about controlling. He made sure she had no friends, no car, and no money. No children either."

"We're not going to waste any time getting home. Transporting cash makes me nervous." Meggie turned the key in the ignition and the engine fired up.

"That makes two of us." Shirley blinked and fidgeted in her seat. "If the fuzz stops us, I wouldn't want to explain why we're hauling a bag of greenbacks in the trunk of this car. Stolen greenbacks at that."

Meggie rolled the driver's window down and pulled away from the curb. At the stop sign she turned left and followed the road signs to High Bridge. On her way she encountered more cars than she had earlier in the day. She glanced at the clock on the dashboard. Rush hour started earlier in Superior.

Meggie spoke little on the way over the bridge and through Duluth. She thought about Amelia's story. The woman must have been desperate to get away from her husband. The money, a godsend.

Once they traveled through the city, Meggie leaned back in her seat and relaxed. An hour away from Duluth, the traffic thinned. Houses dotted the countryside and trees became more abundant. She glanced at the fuel gauge. It showed less than a quarter tank of gas.

"I think I better fill the Bug up," Meggie remarked. "I completely forgot to stop at a gas station on the way out of Duluth." She tapped her finger against the steering wheel. "If I remember right, there's a convenience store just up ahead."

"This stretch of road is sure desolate." Shirley squirmed in her seat and shot Meggie a look. "I'd hate to run out of gas or break down."

Meggie slowed the car, turned left off the two-way road and came to a stop beside the first of two gas pumps. When Shirley went inside, Meggie filled the gas tank, washed the windows then hurried into the store.

A young man stood behind the till. He handed Meggie her change and nodded toward the gray sky. "You drive safe. It looks like there's a storm brewing out there."

Once back on the road, the Bug hummed along. "I'll be glad when we get home." Meggie peered skyward through the windshield. "The clouds look like they're about to burst."

The farther she drove, the fewer houses they passed. Forested areas stretched out for long distances on both sides of the road and were separated only by the occasional field.

After some time, Meggie noticed Shirley had grown quiet and seemed preoccupied about something. "Is anything wrong? You're not talking."

Shirley rubbed her knee and cleared her throat. She turned around and looked out the back window. "I think there's a car following us."

"A car following us?" Meggie creased her brow and glanced at her passenger. "Are you sure?"

Shirley's voice raised an octave. "I'm sure. I remember the white car because it tailgated us over the bridge and made such a racket. When we left the four-lane highway the same car exited right after we did and followed us past the casino. But when you pulled off the road to get gas, it didn't pass by. I watched from inside the store."

"There are a lot of white cars." Meggie glanced in her rearview mirror and narrowed her eyes. A vehicle did appear to be gaining on them. Her stomach rolled. If Shirley was right, there weren't many other cars on the road and only an occasional house. She pushed on the gas pedal.

Shirley lifted herself off the seat and turned around. "It's getting closer."

Meggie checked the rearview mirror for the second time. She could see the contour of the car. "Get the hornet spray. Just in case we need it."

"Hornet spray? Where is it?" Shirley unbuckled her seatbelt and tossed it to the side.

"In the back seat, maybe on the floor." Meggie scraped a hand through her hair.

Shirley turned her head. "I don't see it back here."

"Look under the seat," Meggie ordered. "The car's almost on top of us."

Shirley twisted her body and leaned through the bucket seats. "Hey. I'm stuck." She gyrated back and forth in an attempt to free herself.

"What? Get unstuck and fast." Meggie bent her arm backward and pushed against her friend's back. When that didn't help her, she grasped the seat control, lifted it and pulled her seat forward.

Shirley's mid-section dropped onto the gears and her heels hit the underside of the dashboard. "My neck!" She wailed.

Meggie tried to move Shirley off the gears. "Are you all right?"

"I don't see the hornet spray. It's not back here."

"Check under the seats." Meggie screamed. "Hurry!" The white vehicle sped up and rammed them from behind. The Bug lurched forward. Meggie gasped and pushed on the gas pedal. She tightened her grip on the steering wheel and locked her eyes on the road.

"What's going on?" Shirley wiggled her way out from between the seats and plunked down. She held tight to the can of hornet spray. Her eyes grew large. "He's passing us!"

The vehicle loomed up next to the Bug. Meggie's heart raced. She watched in horror as the white car sideswiped them. The Volkswagen veered to the right, then zigzagged back into the center of the lane.

The vehicle hit the VW again. This time the Bug careened towards the side of the road and into the ditch. Meggie clung to the steering wheel and bumped along the ditch bottom. She tried to dodge a large boulder but it scraped the bottom of the Bug.

"Here it comes again," Shirley shouted. The white car plunged into the ditch after them. It moved past them, swung sideways and jerked to a stop in front of the Bug. Meggie hit the steering wheel and Shirley was flung forward in her seat.

Seconds later Meggie opened her eyes. She felt nauseous. Shirley moaned in the seat beside her and rubbed the back of her neck.

A slight scruffy-looking man jumped out of the white vehicle in front of them and ran towards the Volkswagen.

"Give me the spray," Meggie ordered and grabbed the hornet spray from Shirley. Her hands trembled. She removed the cap and tossed it on the floor of the vehicle.

"Get out of the car. You're coming with me." The pistol's barrel pointed at Shirley through the passenger window. "Move it," the man shouted and waved the gun.

Shirley stumbled out of the car. He grabbed her by the arm and looked over his shoulder at Meggie. "Follow me in your car and don't try anything funny or shorty here is dead."

Meggie followed the other car out of the ditch and onto a side road. Her mind whirled. What did he want with them? The money? Where was he taking them?

The white vehicle turned onto a narrow dirt road and into a wooded area. Meggie's stomach churned. What did he plan to do with them?

Red brake lights flashed. The driver's door on the white car swung open. The scruffy looking man jumped out of the car. He turned towards Shirley, mouthed something and rushed toward the Bug.

Meggie climbed out of her vehicle. She stood behind the open driver's door and hid the hornet spray behind her. Her heart thumped. Her legs shook.

The man brushed his black shoulder length hair away from his face and snarled at Meggie. She couldn't make out what he said. Her ears rang and her head ached. She raised the hornet spray, aimed and pushed the button. The jet spray hit its mark.

The man screamed. He dropped his gun and pawed at his eyes. Meggie charged. She knocked the man to the ground and picked up his weapon. He yelped and writhed on the ground.

"He had this in the car," Shirley shouted to Meggie. A rope dangled from her hand. She plunked down on the culprit's legs and handed the rope to Meggie. "I'll sit on him while you tie his hands."

Meggie set the gun aside and knelt down. She wrestled the man's hands away from his face, wrapped the rope around them and tied a secure knot. She stretched out the rope but it came up short. "We'll have to bend his knees to tie his feet."

With Shirley's help they rolled him over, bent his knees and slung the end of the rope around them. By the time they were done he looked like a calf at a rodeo trussed up backwards.

Meggie picked up the gun and handed it to Shirley, then ran to the Bug to search for her cell phone. She found it underneath the seat. The screen read no service. She scuttled back to where the man lay on the ground. He still whimpered. She almost felt sorry for him. Almost.

"One of us will have to drive out to the highway and call for help," she said. "There's no service here. Do you want to go or stay?"

Shirley bit her lip and looked at the thug on the ground. "Will the Bug make it to the highway? If it breaks down, I would have to walk." She sat a moment in thought. "You go, I'll stay."

"If he gives you trouble, shoot him—hornet spray or gun—your choice."

This last remark elicited a scream from the man. Shirley ordered him to shut up if he knew what was good for him. She nodded for Meggie to leave.

The Bug's engine wouldn't turn over. Meggie slapped the steering wheel. The VW blocked the white car. And too many trees prevented her from driving the other car around the Bug. She had no choice but to start hiking.

Every so often Meggie tried her cell phone, but no bars. She ran a short distance, stopped and tried her cell again. This time she connected with 911. Minutes later sirens wailed in the distance. She peered down the highway. Flashing lights came into view.

The highway patrol car came to an abrupt stop behind the Bug. The patrol officer closed the vehicle door and made his way to the man on the ground.

Meggie clambered out of the passenger seat. She motioned Shirley aside. "Did he say anything?"

Shirley leaned in close to Meggie. "He told me the gun I had aimed at him was a fake. Good thing I had the hornet spray." She held her hand out. "I found this in his wallet."

Meggie looked at the identification card. "Fake gun? Darrell Schmidt is all bark and no bite."

Shirley whispered. "What are you going to tell them about the money?"

Meggie tapped her index finger against her lip and studied Darrell Schmidt. "If he doesn't mention the money to them, I'm not saying anything. I promised Amelia I'd give it to Bulldog." She eyed Shirley. "I don't think that's a crime. It's not like we're withholding evidence or anything."

CHAPTER 19

A FTER THE DEPUTY TOOK MEGGIE'S statement, she stopped by the glass-enclosed reception area and inquired if Bulldog would be in the next day. The woman at the desk confirmed he would be in and jotted her name in the appointment book.

That taken care of, she walked to the large window that faced the parking area and looked for Shirley's car. When she didn't see the Taurus, she knew her friend had finished giving her statement to the officer and had gone home. Shirley had offered to wait with her until Walter arrived to pick her up, but Meggie had declined the offer.

Meggie turned away from the window and sat in a chair to wait for Walter. She had no idea what kind of mood he would be in, but she guessed it wouldn't be a good one. She thought about the Bug. Her hands had been tied. It would have been much simpler to have it towed to the garage, but not with a trunk full of stolen money.

Tomorrow she would hand over the bag of money to Bulldog. Amelia had been adamant about dealing with him. She met Bulldog when she posted bail for her husband during her turbulent marriage and never forgot his kindness. Of all the law enforcement officials, she chose to confide in Bulldog. Good cop, bad cop all rolled into one.

She gazed out the window at the sky. In a matter of minutes the sun would set, and she would be doing her chores in the dark. She rubbed her neck then jumped to her feet when Walter's truck pulled up in front of the Law Enforcement Center.

She pushed the glass door wide and strode out to the truck. "Hi, honey. Thanks for coming." She crawled into the passenger seat, buckled her seatbelt and gave her husband a big smile. "I know you're wondering what this is all about."

Walter turned towards her with a pained look on his face. "I'm wondering all right. But I'm almost one hundred and one percent sure I'm not going to like what I hear." He turned out of the parking lot and headed in the direction of Highway 52. "And before you ask, I have the tow rope in the back of the pickup and my pajama bag in the back seat." He glanced over at Meggie. "Now, what is this all about?"

After Meggie finished explaining to Walter what happened, she leaned back in the passenger seat while he ranted on and on. He wasted no time in letting her know how he felt about her harebrained trip to Superior. He emphasized the fact that he warned her not to get involved in trying to find out what happened to Amelia.

By the time the Bug pulled into Rileys' driveway, the sun had sunk below the horizon and Meggie's mood right along with it. Walter's mood, on the other hand, had not changed since he picked her up at the Law Enforcement Center. His bad mood stayed the course.

She crawled out of the truck and waited for Walter in front of the vehicle. He rolled up the truck windows, slammed the driver's door and pressed the remote. "I better lock the doors. You never know who might trespass tonight and steal something. Heaven knows you're a magnet for trouble."

She took his hand in hers and gazed up at him. "Don't be mad. Everything's going to work out fine. Trust me."

He shook his head and followed her into the house. "You're probably right. What could possibly go wrong that already hasn't?"

THE NEXT MORNING, MEGGIE pulled the vinyl bag out from under the bed, carried it outside and set it in the front seat of the truck. She walked to the back of the pickup and found Walter bent over the truck's tow bar and attempting to attach it to the Bug.

"I'm going to run and do the chores while you're hooking up the VW. It won't take me long. Have another cup of coffee if you finish before me." Walter grunted so she took that as an okay and hurried off to do the chores.

Only half her mind concentrated on her duties. The other half dwelled on all that had taken place in the last twenty-four hours. Darrell Schmidt had deliberately run them off the road for the bag of money. He must have known where Ruth Burnson lived or followed her there. But how did he know she planned to drive to Superior?

Porky lifted his snout and snorted at her. Evidently, she wasn't moving fast enough for him. She lifted the padlock off the kennel door and glared at him as he wobbled in front of her. Pushy pig.

Once the horses were in the pasture, Meggie ran back to the house. She found Walter in the kitchen drinking a cup of coffee and eating another caramel roll. He shoved the last bite in his mouth when he saw her come in.

"You ready?" He tipped up his coffee mug and set it on the table. "Let's do it."

Walter didn't say much on the way into Pine Lake. He drove slow and kept his eyes focused on the rearview mirror.

Meggie turned around to check on the Bug every few minutes. "Thanks for doing this. Do you think they'll loan me a car while they're fixing mine?" She spread cream over her hands. The scent of lavender filled the cab.

"Andy usually keeps a loaner at the shop. I'm sure you'll qualify as long as someone else isn't using it." Walter glanced at his wife. "If worse comes to worst, I'll stay with you at the farm until the Bug gets fixed."

Meggie thanked him and appreciated his concern. She hoped it wouldn't come to that since he wouldn't feel comfortable in someone else's recliner. Besides that, Riley's television set didn't compare to his big screen TV.

A short time later Meggie drove out of Andy's Autos in a yellow Jeep. It wasn't the greatest looking vehicle, but it would serve the purpose. She looked at the bag of money on the seat beside her and thought about what she would say to Bulldog.

Meggie switched the radio on, but soon realized she couldn't hear anything over the engine's noise. She switched it back off. By the time she turned off the street and into the Law Enforcement Center parking lot, her heart felt like it would burst out of her chest.

The visitor's lot appeared full, so she drove around to the back of the building. There she found an empty parking spot and pulled in. She sat in the car a moment and rehearsed what she would tell Detective Peterson. Her stomach turned at the thought of meeting with him, but there was no getting around it. She had to explain how she came to be in possession of stolen money.

Meggie steepled her fingers, took a deep breath and counted to ten. Then slung her purse over her shoulder and hoisted the bag of money off the front seat. With vinyl bag in hand, she held her head high and walked into the Law Enforcement Center.

Inside the building she set the bag on the floor, lowered herself into a chair and waited for Bulldog to arrive. She wanted to flee, but instead stood and paced. She sat back down. A few minutes later Bulldog's truck pulled into the parking lot.

Meggie's knee bounced up and down as the minutes ticked by. Finally, Bulldog opened the lobby door and lumbered over to her. "Meggie, come on back." He eyed the dirty vinyl bag but didn't ask about it. Instead he smiled and led her through the work area and into his office.

Bulldog closed the door. He walked around his desk and sat down in his chair. "What can I do for you this morning, Meggie?"

"I'm not here for myself." She cleared her throat. "Shirley and I were in yesterday to give a statement regarding a man that tried to run us off the road. I presume he's sitting in jail now."

When Bulldog didn't respond she continued. "I believe he ran us off the road because he wanted this." She bent over, lifted the bag of money off the floor and passed it across the desk to the detective.

Bulldog's eyebrows narrowed as he reached for the dirty vinyl bag. He set it down on his lap and unzipped it. His eyebrows shot up and he let out a low whistle. Seconds later he set the bag beside his chair on the floor and leaned his elbows on the table. "You better explain."

"It's a long story."

"It usually is, but I have all the time you need." He reached for the recorder and set it down in the center of the desk. "I'll have to record this conversation." He turned the recorder on and nodded at Meggie to begin.

She told Bulldog how she learned about Amelia's sister and why she tried to find her. "I thought if I could find Ruth Burnson alive she might know something about Amelia's disappearance. Otherwise, why wouldn't she have filed a missing persons report?" She paused. "And I discovered some letters at the farm that Amelia had written and wanted to return them to her. That is, if I found her alive."

By the time she finished her statement and the recorder had been switched off, Bulldog sat stone-faced in his chair. "And she wants to meet with me?"

"Amelia trusts you," Meggie's heart palpitated. "She's afraid she might have to go to prison. She dug the money up after Darrell buried it, but she didn't steal it from the bank. She only spent enough to buy a bus ticket to Superior. She had to get away from her abusive husband, but had no money to buy a ticket."

Meggie caught her breath and nodded at the vinyl bag. "She paid the money back. The fact that her step-grandson, Darrell Schmidt, tried to run us off the road to get that money proves he knew about the money."

Bulldog held up his hand. "Whoa, slow down. I'm receiving an overload of information here." He scratched his chin. "Listen. I don't know what'll happen to Amelia after she confesses. My gut feeling tells me they won't send her to prison. Regardless, she needs to come in as soon as possible and give us a statement."

He picked up a pencil and tapped it against the desk. "Why do you suppose Darrell Schmidt knew enough to follow you to Superior?"

"I've wondered about that." Meggie thought a minute. "Shirley and I were in the horse pasture the night he came back for the money. At least, I assume it was him. We watched him digging from the top of the hill. I think he knew we were there."

Her eyes squinted. "And I'm pretty sure he broke into Rileys' house and searched the attic for the stash. Even so, he wouldn't have known anything about our plans to go to Superior because we hadn't made them yet."

Bulldog bowed his head and rubbed his temples.

Meggie suspected she had given him a headache but that didn't deter her. "No one else knew we planned to drive to Superior, not even Walter or Bill. We didn't talk about our plans in public . . ." She paused and wrinkled her brow, "Except the night before we left when we were at the meat raffle."

Bulldog lifted his head and made eye contact with Meggie. "Do you think someone at the Legion Club overheard you and Shirley making plans?"

Meggie took her time before she answered his question. "An older man was sitting at the table next to us, but I don't think we were talking loud enough for him to hear anything. I don't know his name." She recalled that the man leaned towards their table. At the time she thought he had too many beers. Could he have been eavesdropping?

Bulldog peered at Meggie, his smile appeared tight.

"We could have been talking loud enough, I guess."

On her way back to the farm past events replayed in Meggie's mind. She thought about Darrell Schmidt and wondered how he ended up in Superior. Everything else he did fell into place except that. Whatever the reason, greed had put him in prison once and greed would send him back again.

CHAPTER 20

SEVERAL DAYS LATER, MEGGIE sat in Pine Lake Café and stirred her raspberry tea. She recalled the day she had lunch with Shirley and Audrey and announced her plans to housesit the hobby farm. So much had happened since then. Molly had said her goodbyes to Michael and had returned home. Meggie had crossed another item off her bucket list.

"It didn't do Darrell much good to turn state's evidence against his partner in order to get a shorter sentence." Shirley squirted more catsup on her French fries and popped one into her mouth. "He gets out of prison, pulls a few stupid stunts and ends up back in the slammer."

Meggie dipped her roast beef sandwich into the rich brown au jus. She raised the sandwich to her mouth, took a big bite and savored the taste. After several seconds she wiped her hands on her napkin and focused on Shirley.

"Keep in mind how desperate he must have been when they released him from prison. He probably spent all those years incarcerated thinking about the money he had buried."

"And when he didn't find it, he went looking for it," Audrey said. "I don't understand why he thought Fred took it."

Meggie slid her plate to the side and sipped her drink. "Through a process of elimination, he must have come to the conclusion Fred had taken it. His father wasn't home when he buried it. He knew Amelia had been in bed. That left Fred."

Audrey's brows narrowed. "Why, Fred? He buried it at night, didn't he? What would Fred be doing out at night in that area?"

"Fred liked to ride his horse at night. I suppose Darrell thought it possible he had been riding and witnessed him burying it."

"That's why Meggie thinks he broke into Riley's house." Shirley chewed on her burger and swallowed. "But from what we've heard, he won't admit to breaking in."

"What do you mean by 'I think' he broke into Riley's house?"

"Are you positive about the intruder? Maybe you were dreaming or just imagined someone in the attic."

"Of course I'm sure. I wasn't dreaming, drunk or hallucinating. You know me better than that. Besides, there were footprints in the attic's dusty floor and on the stairs."

Audrey tilted her head. "For argument's sake, let's say he did break into Riley's house. Why did he think he would find the money there after all these years?"

Meggie's eyes gleamed. "Fred was reported missing after Darrell was arrested. Perhaps Darrell figured Fred dug up the bag of money and hid it until he could turn it over to the authorities. But since that never happened and it was never found . . ."

"Darrell might have believed Fred hid it in the attic or staircase. He knew him to be an honest man who wouldn't run away with stolen money. It was a longshot." Shirley jutted her chin. "Who knows? Maybe Darrell suspected his grandfather had done away with both Amelia and Fred. From what we hear, Darrell denies having anything to do with Fred's disappearance. He liked Fred."

The waitress appeared at their table and asked if anyone would like dessert. Meggie ordered a butterscotch sundae and Shirley, pecan pie. Audrey passed on dessert.

As soon as the waitress turned away Audrey leaned over the table toward Meggie. "I don't understand how Darrell knew you were driving to Superior?"

Meggie bit her lip and Shirley shifted in her seat. "That would probably be our fault," Meggie admitted. "We should have known better, but we discussed our plans the night of the meat raffle. Later we learned that Herman Schmidt, Darrell's grandfather, sat at the table next to ours and heard everything."

Shirley touched the scarf at her neck. "I imagine he told his grandson what we discussed, and Darrell followed us to Superior. Did he plan to confront Amelia if we found her? We don't know. But then he saw us walk out of the assisted-living facility with that vinyl bag. You know the rest of the story."

LATER THAT WEEK, MEGGIE slid the glass door closed behind her and carried her coffee outside. A chipmunk in the far corner of the deck swiveled to attention. It darted across the deck, scurried down the steps and out of sight.

She brushed the lounge chair off and sat down. It felt good to be home in Pine Lake, although she missed the hobby farm. She wouldn't miss mucking the stalls or chasing pigs in the rain, but she didn't regret taking the job. Molly had been so grateful to her. She had been able to spend quality time with her husband, Michael. That in itself made it all worthwhile.

The morning sun sparkled through the leaves on the birch tree. They quivered in the gentle breeze. A chickadee sat on the edge of the cabin bird feeder, darted its head from side to side and flew off.

The glass door slid open and Walter stuck his head out. "Are you ready to go?"

Meggie looked at her watch and gasped. "I had no idea it was so late. I'll only be a minute." She had forgotten Walter had volunteered to help out at the Legion Club in Bluff.

She grabbed her coffee cup and hurried into the house. On the table lay the sympathy card addressed to Fred Jackson's family. She picked it up and slipped it into her purse.

In the bedroom she lifted the navy blue dress off the ironing board and slid it over her shoulders. She found her dress sandals near the back of the closet and slipped them on.

A few minutes later, Walter crawled into the Bug's passenger seat. He rolled the window all the way down and set his elbow on the car's door. "It's not fair that a good man like Fred Jackson ended up the way he did. From what I hear, he would have taken the shirt off his back for anyone. But then life isn't always fair, is it?"

"At least Fred'll have a proper burial now. I'm sure it must have been difficult for those close to him to find out he spent so many years at the bottom of a well."

There were few cars in the parking lot when Meggie and Walter arrived at the Legion Club. She took her husband's hand and together they started across the parking lot.

Several men in military uniform gathered inside the club. Meggie hung back while her husband walked over and spoke with one of them. The man pointed Walter towards a large room on the left.

While waiting for Walter, Meggie found her way to the kitchen area. The ding of pots and pans and a low hum of conversation escaped the shutters over the counter. She knocked on the closed door and peeked in. Savory smells permeated the small room. One woman bustled about and smiled. "What can I do for you?"

"I'm offering my services if you need any help."

The woman thanked her and said most of the work was done.

Meggie backed out of the kitchen. She milled around and spotted a basket on the table near the microphone. She opened her purse, pulled out the sympathy card for Fred's family and dropped it in the basket. After signing the guest book, she sat down in the back of the room and waited for Walter.

LATER THAT MORNING, the VW climbed Bluff Hill Road and followed the curvy lane to the cemetery. Inside the cemetery gates the bugler and color guard stood several yards away from the gravesite. The firing party stood ready and in full view of the family.

She followed the lane through the cemetery, pulled the Bug over and parked under the shade of a large oak tree. Dappled light shone on the ground. The scent of fresh mown grass hung in the air.

A number of folding chairs were set up near the open grave. Several mourners gathered close by. Amelia Schmidt stood next to a man and rested her hand on his arm. They appeared to be in deep conversation.

Three mourners stood apart from the others and hovered in the background. The younger woman said something to the older woman, then walked over to join the man conversing with Amelia Schmidt.

Low-key conversation buzzed until all heads turned toward the cemetery's entrance. A hearse pulled up near the gravesite. The driver's door opened and the funeral director stepped out. He walked to the back of the vehicle and unlocked the rear door of the hearse.

The pallbearers carried Fred's remains to his wife's gravesite. They held the flag over the urn and the service began. The minister led the mourners in prayer and asked, "Would anyone like to say a few words about Mr. Jackson?"

Barry Jackson, Fred's nephew, introduced himself. The tall good-looking man thanked everyone for attending the service and said a few words about his uncle's character. An elderly man in uniform remembered Fred's patriotism. When they finished speaking, the funeral director asked the mourners to stand for the rendering of honors. Volleys were fired and "Taps" sounded.

Meggie and Walter stood near the back of the mourners while family and close friends occupied the folding chairs. A tear formed in Meggie's eye as she watched the military detail fold the American flag over the cremation urn, hand it to the detail assistant, who in turn passed it to the detail leader. The detail leader presented the flag to the man who had been speaking with Amelia, Fred's nephew.

The minister announced that lunch would be served at the American Legion Club in Bluff. Condolences were offered, and one by one the mourners left the gravesite. A handful of those closest to Fred remained. Meggie turned to Walter. "Let's go, shall we?"

The drive to Bluff Legion Club proved somber. Meggie wondered if Fred's service reminded her husband of his father's military funeral. She tried to converse with Walter, but soon realized he didn't want to talk. She left him alone with his reflections and drove on in silence.

When they arrived at the Legion Club, several people from the cemetery were standing outside the front door visiting. Inside the building, a number of people gathered around the bar area.

Meggie followed Walter into the reserved room, sat down next to him at a table and waited until the family arrived. She heard her name and turned to see Amelia Schmidt standing by her side. Ruth Burnson stood next to her.

Meggie slid her chair back and rose. "Please sit down. I'm so glad you didn't leave right after the services. We didn't have a chance to talk earlier." She pulled a chair out for each of them and waited until they sat down.

"I wouldn't leave Bluff without thanking you. I owe you so much." Amelia grinned. "I had a nice talk with Lars and he told me there would be a court hearing. For the time being they released me on my own recognizance." An inner light shone in her eyes. "I suppose they don't think an old lady like me will try to make a run for it."

Meggie expressed relief that everything seemed to be turning out in a good way. Their conversation was cut short when voices rose in the bar room. Heads turned toward the commotion.

Barry Jackson, Fred's nephew, had arrived. He made his way through the mourners, greeted many and shook hands with several. The young woman who sat next to him at the gravesite linked her arm in his. He appeared to be introducing her around. After several minutes he made his way into the private room.

"That's Barry's daughter, Michelle, a pretty young woman. She lives with her mother in the city near Barry," Amelia whispered. "His ex-wife, Jacqueline, and her brother, Simon, were at the gravesite services, but I don't see them here."

Barry and Michelle strode towards the front of the room where the luncheon had been set out. They picked up their plates and started to move through the buffet line. Guests took their cue and fell in behind them.

After everyone at Meggie's table returned from the lunch line, Meggie noticed Ruth and Amelia did not have a beverage. She offered to get them one. When she came back to the table, Barry and his daughter were seated with the others.

Barry stood as she approached the table. He waited until she set the beverages in front of Amelia and Ruth then held out his hand and smiled. "We haven't met. I'm Fred's nephew, Barry Jackson." He turned to the young woman sitting next to him. "This is my daughter, Michelle. We owe you a debt of gratitude for finding my uncle. Molly Riley has high praise for you."

Meggie accepted his thanks and expressed her condolences. Conversation centered around Fred and life on the farm. Barry admitted he didn't spend as much time with Fred as he would have liked, but recalled a funny story or two about his visits to the farm. When there was a lull in the conversation, Walter excused himself and left the table.

"They want to talk to me down at the sheriff's office," Barry commented. "They're investigating Uncle Fred's murder. Close relatives are always suspected until they're cleared." He ran his finger around his coffee cup. "I'm Uncle Fred's only nephew. He had few relatives."

Michelle's face fell. "I'm sure they think because the house was in your name, too, that you might have had motive to do harm to Uncle Fred."

"I'm not worried," Barry rushed his words. "I didn't have a thing to do with his death."

After Barry and Michelle left the table, Amelia confided to Meggie that Barry told her his divorce was anything but amicable. Evidently his wife, Jacqueline, had taken him to the cleaners. "What with the sale of the farm and half of everything else he owned, she came out smelling like a rose." Amelia glanced toward the doorway. "There she is now with her brother. Simon helped Fred on the farm every now and then when he lived near Bluff."

A hush fell over the crowd when the tall attractive woman walked in. She glanced around, whispered something to her brother and proceeded through the buffet line. She nodded at Barry, who stood nearby, then sat down at an empty table.

Simon walked with a limp and trailed behind her. He seemed like a fish out of water and darted furtive looks here and there.

Something niggled at the back of Meggie's mind, but she couldn't put her finger on it. Her eyes narrowed. After a moment it hit her. Maud, the librarian, had suspected a hired hand with a limp might have done away with Fred. Could that man possibly be Simon? Did he have a motive to kill Fred?

Barry Jackson had a motive. He would be sole owner of the farm. But did he have the opportunity?

CHAPTER 21

A SHRILL RING WOKE MEGGIE. She fumbled for the bedside phone.

"Meggie, I'm sorry to bother you," Vera's voice quivered. "Eldon fell during the night. He's in the hospital."

Meggie sat up in bed. "What can I do?"

"I'm dreadfully worried about him. I know he would appreciate it if I were by his side." She paused a moment and caught her breath. "Could you possibly look after the shop for me today? I don't want to put you out. If you can't make it, I'll understand."

"Don't worry about the shop. I'll get dressed right now. Eldon needs you."

MEGGIE ARRIVED AT HEARTS and Flowers to find Vera in a dither. She paced back and forth across the tiled floor and darted glances out the front window of the shop. "I'm so relieved you're here, Meggie. I've been beside myself with worry." Her voice faltered. "Nettie's due here any minute to drive me to the hospital."

Meggie heard a low rumble. She turned and glanced out the window. Nettie's car screeched to a halt in front of the shop. Its right front tire nearly hit the curb, her idea of parallel parking.

"There she is now," Vera exclaimed. "Thank you so much for watching my little shop."

Meggie followed Vera out to the car. After greeting Nettie, she turned to Vera, "Say hello to Eldon for me. Tell him to get better soon. He has a wedding to go to!" She stepped away from the curb and folded her arms.

Nettie ground the gears. The car lurched forward. She braked, reversed and squealed away from the curb. Seconds later she stuck her hand out the driver's window and waved over the top of the car.

Meggie shook her head and shuddered. She glanced around to see who else witnessed Nettie's bizarre driving. Thank heavens there were few people on the street. Had the time finally come for someone to speak to Nettie about relinquishing her driver's license? For all the good it would do.

After the car disappeared from sight, she walked back into the shop and turned the sign on the door to let the public know Hearts and Flowers Gift Shop was open for business.

LATER THAT MORNING, the bell tinkled over the door, and two mature women breezed in. They spent several minutes inspecting merchandise, made a mess of Nettie's crocheted pillowcases and walked back out. Meggie straightened the goods. She yawned and looked up at the wall clock. The morning dragged on.

By afternoon Meggie had accomplished several tasks in the shop, received a report from Vera regarding Eldon's broken leg and fielded several calls from would-be customers. Now perched on the stool behind the counter, she jotted notes to herself.

The phone rang and echoed through the shop. She grabbed it on the second ring and recognized Molly Riley's voice.

"I'm sorry to bother you at work but when I called your house Walter told me it would be all right to call you at the shop."

Meggie brushed aside her apology and slid off the stool. "It's been slow here this morning. You say you have some sort of emergency? Are you all right?"

"I'm fine but I can't say the same for my yellow lab. That's why I'm calling. I think I told you about that lump I found on him? Well, I took him to the vet, and he is going to need surgery." She went on to explain that Brandy would spend the night after surgery in the animal hospital and then return home to recuperate.

"It's a lot to ask after everything you went through when you housesat before, but would you want to sit one more night? I arrived at work this morning and found out I'm scheduled to work the first night Brandy comes home from the hospital. I don't want to leave her alone."

Meggie slid her reading glasses on. She jotted down the date of Brandy's surgery, the time she would need to arrive at the farm and the time Molly would return home the following morning.

When she checked her appointment calendar, she found she had nothing pressing to do for most of that day. "I'm free that afternoon and evening. I might have to help Vera that morning in the shop, but I won't know for sure until I speak with her. Either way, I would love to visit the farm again and watch over Brandy."

Molly thanked her profusely and suggested that perhaps Shirley would like to join her since she had expressed an interest in riding Beauty again. When Meggie agreed to the idea, Molly promised to extend an invitation to Shirley.

A few minutes later the phone rang. Meggie wasn't surprised to find Shirley on the other end of the line. Her friend admitted she would love to ride Beauty again, but expressed concern about staying overnight. At the same time she didn't want to hurt Molly's feelings.

Meggie downplayed Shirley's fear of ghosts and laughed at the possibility that a ghost would attach itself to her. She found it unlikely anything unpleasant would happen while they were at the farm.

After a certain amount of coaxing, Shirley changed her mind. "I really would love to ride Beauty again. I told Bill if we were younger I would have him buy me a horse. He just laughed."

Following some discussion, plans were made. Meggie laid the phone in its cradle and breathed a sigh of relief. She wouldn't have to spend the night alone at the farm. She admitted that some of Shirley's fears were founded. She would be the last person to tell her that.

SEVERAL DAYS LATER, when the yellow farmhouse came into view, Meggie experienced déjà vu. A brief glimpse from the past flitted through her mind—flashbacks of a white horse, the smell of Old Spice and cigars, cold air swirling around her. She quivered and for an instant wanted to turn the car around and go home.

Meggie pressed a fist against her mouth and reprimanded herself. She wouldn't waste another minute on worry. Instead she would rid her mind of unpleasant thoughts and focus on the blue sky, sunshine and green fields. Nothing would blemish her visit. Besides, she wouldn't be spending the night alone.

"I don't see Black and Beauty in the side pasture," Shirley blurted out. "I hope they're nearby. At the very least, I hope they've learned to come when called. Look, there's Molly now."

Meggie braked the car in front of the farmhouse. The pretty young woman held her hand up to stop the car. She laid the broom down, brushed her long brown hair out of her face and hurried towards them.

Her lips curved into a smile as she leaned into the driver's window. "Hello. You can park in the garage if you'd like. I've spent hours this week cleaning it. Now there's actually room for a vehicle."

"That sounds like a good idea." Meggie slapped a mosquito on her arm. "I heard the weather report this morning. They're predicting heavy rain and hail later today." When Molly stepped away from the Bug, Meggie shifted the car into reverse and backed into the garage.

The building had definitely been given a face lift. Michael's tools were gathered together, organized and mounted above the work bench. All leftover odds and ends from remodeling were gone and the entire cement floor appeared to have been washed. The old hutch sat in the same spot but no paraphernalia surrounded it.

"Sure looks different, doesn't it?" Molly followed them into the garage. "Michael will go into shock when he sees it."

"You don't have to tell me how much work goes into cleaning a garage." Shirley lifted her bag out of the car and ambled towards Molly. "I don't clean our garage anymore. I figure if Bill messes it, he cleans it."

Molly laughed. "I'm glad you're both here. Not only because Brandy needs a sitter. I really enjoy company. It gets lonely way out here at times." She glanced at their luggage. "Can I help you carry anything?" When they declined, she led the way to the house.

A woodpecker knocked its beak against a rotted pine tree. Their host acknowledged the red-headed bird. "Thanks heavens for wild birds and farm animals." She nodded at the hummingbird feeder suspended from the porch eaves. "Even those tiny birds are a godsend."

Meggie watched a tiny bird suck nectar from the feeder and thought about Molly's reluctance to be alone on the farm.

"When I first suspected this house might be haunted I was afraid. But I wouldn't admit my fears to anyone. Over time I learned to live with the situation. But when Fred Jackson was found in the well, my old fears set in." She paused. "The solitude has become almost unbearable. I pray every day Michael will find work closer to home."

Meggie tried to think of something reassuring to say, but Molly changed the subject and continued on.

"I'll be leaving early for the hospital to cover for a co-worker who needs to take off early. I'll probably be napping when you return from riding. I don't want to fall asleep at the wheel." Molly pulled the screen door open and motioned her guests into the entryway. "Shirley, you can have either bedroom upstairs, whichever you prefer. They're both ready." She glanced down at Shirley's bag and held out her hand. "Are you sure I can't help you with that?"

Shirley shook her head. "No thanks. I can manage. It's not heavy."

Molly drew her hand back and watched Shirley climb the stairs. "As soon as you're settled in, come down for some lunch."

In the master bedroom Brandy slept on a mat near the head of the bed, her food and water dish nearby.

"I hope you don't mind if you share the room with a dog." Molly shifted her eyes from Meggie to Brandy. "I thought it made more sense to have her in the bedroom than anyplace else. She might wake during the night. If she slept in another area, you probably wouldn't hear her."

Meggie assured Molly she had no qualms about sharing the bedroom with man's best friend. She admitted to feeling safer with Brandy close by.

"Thanks, Meggie. I really appreciate what you're doing." A smile spread across the young woman's face and her eyes rested on Brandy. "The vet told me she would sleep most of the day and into the evening. She's gone through a lot."

Shirley crept into the bedroom and stood beside the other women. Brandy moaned and twitched, but her eyes remained closed. "I don't think she'll be much company tonight, but maybe she'll keep any unwanted visitors away, if you know what I mean."

Meggie nudged Shirley. She widened her eyes and shook her head slightly in an attempt to warn her friend against mentioning the strange happenings that had taken place on the farm. The less Molly thought about them the better.

The three women crept out of the bedroom and Molly closed the door behind them. "I hope you don't mind sleeping upstairs, Shirley." She slipped an apron on and began pulling dishes out of the cupboard. "After all that's happened I wouldn't blame you if you did." She turned to her guests. "Make yourselves at home. It'll only be a minute. I hope you're hungry."

Shirley cleared her throat and crossed her fingers behind her back. "Don't think for a minute that I'm worried about ghosts. The thought never crossed my mind. I couldn't have been more excited when you invited me to spend the night."

CHAPTER 22

M EGGIE SAT DOWN at the kitchen table to enjoy the light lunch Molly prepared earlier that morning. A small vase of pansies sat in the center of the kitchen table and brightened up the occasion.

Their hostess poured three glasses of iced tea and then passed around a small bowl of lemon slices. She encouraged them to eat as much as they wanted and mentioned a pan of lasagna in the refrigerator for their supper.

Soon after sitting down, the subject of Michael's job came up. Molly talked about the oil boom in North Dakota, what Michael actually did on the job and how he landed it in the first place. "So although he makes good money working for the oil company, he misses home. He's hoping to find employment in the area so he can move back here."

Shirley kept the conversation lively with her rendition of Bill and Walter's annual fishing trip to the cabin on Gopher Lake in northern Minnesota. "I don't understand their idea of fun. They hole up in a cabin in the sticks and do nothing but fish." She helped herself to more fruit salad and elicited laughs when she said, "Fruit salad with real whipped cream. I'm starting my diet on Monday."

"Meggie, I can't tell you how surprised I felt when you told me about the secret staircase. When I told Michael what you discovered, he couldn't believe it." Molly lifted her glass of iced tea, took a sip and set it back down on the table.

"I know it sounds crazy that we never discovered the secret passageway ourselves. But in all honesty, we seldom go upstairs and we rarely have guests." She picked up her pork sandwich and bit into it. "And remember, we purchased the house long before we used it as a residence. It served as a weekend getaway for some time."

Meggie thought about Fred and how he disguised the panel door in the bedroom wall. "Building a small bookcase over the panel took some doing," she said. "I really admire Fred's handiwork. Amelia told me he liked to tinker around and come up with unusual ideas."

She realized Molly didn't know the full details about the discovery of the hidden staircase and what led up to it. She proceeded to fill her in. When she finished her tale, she set her napkin on the table. ". . . and if I hadn't been checking out the attic, we still wouldn't know it existed."

"That is quite a story. We're so pleased you made the discovery."

Molly asked if anyone would like more tea. Both women nodded. She refilled their glasses and encouraged them to have another brownie while she cleared the dirty lunch dishes off the table.

When she returned to the table, she sat down and picked up a brownie from the desert plate. "Anyway, I've been waiting to tell you something you'll both find interesting." Her eyes sparkled. "After I returned home, I checked all the stairs to see if there were any more hiding places. Guess what I discovered?"

Meggie's stomach fluttered. She set her iced tea down on the table and waited in suspense to hear what Molly would say.

"After all my searching, and I mean every stair in this house, I didn't find any more secret hiding places but I did find . . ."

Shirley's eyes lit up. "Tell me you found something that will point to Fred's killer."

A heavy sigh escaped Molly. "I wish I could tell you the name of the person who murdered Fred, but I can't. But I can tell you I discovered a key in the stair where you found the letters. It had gotten stuck in a crack."

"That's interesting." Meggie's gaze focused on Molly. "Did you let Barry know what you found?"

Molly nodded and stated she called Barry the same day she found the key. He had no idea what the key belonged to. Although he figured it probably was garbage, he asked her to drop it in the mail. Molly's face tightened. "I wondered if sending it in the mail would be taking a chance. What if the key turned out to be for something important and it was lost in the mail?"

"Maybe Fred had cash stashed somewhere in a locker," Shirley babbled. "Or maybe he had other valuables hidden away."

"It doesn't matter because I didn't send it." Molly looked sheepish and rubbed her finger up and down her glass of iced tea. "Actually, I forgot all about it until I cleaned out that hutch in the garage yesterday. I came across some old photographs and a few paper documents."

Molly went on to say she called Barry earlier in the day to let him know about the photos and documents. He wasn't home but she spoke with his daughter who happened to be at his house visiting. "I asked her to tell Barry I'd box up the key along with the photographs and documents and get them in the mail tomorrow." Molly nodded to the package on the table.

The conversation turned to the history of Fred's antique hutch and why Molly and Michael had it in their garage after all these years. "I'm embarrassed to say I planned to refinish it early on, but I just haven't found the time." Molly sucked on a piece of ice then bit into it. "When I returned home from North Dakota I promised myself I would finish the job and move it back into the house."

A few minutes later she pushed her chair back and stood up. "You two better hurry if you plan to ride the horses. I kept them in the corral this morning so you wouldn't have to look for them." She glanced out the window. "You never know how long this weather will hold out."

LATER THAT EVENING after Molly left for work, the women rested on the front porch. The floor creaked beneath their rocking chairs. The wind chime tinkled. Both women seemed lost in thought.

"It's interesting, isn't it?"

"What are you talking about?" Shirley scowled and popped a last piece of brownie into her mouth. "Did you know you have a really bad habit?"

Meggie laughed and turned her head toward her friend. "I'm not sure what you're referring to, but I have no doubt you're going to tell me."

"You think about something, blurt it out and expect me to know what you're talking about."

Meggie leaned her head back and chuckled. "You're right. I'm guilty as charged. Walter has accused me of the same thing." She paused a moment. "I've been thinking about the hutch and the fact that it's still on the farm after all these years."

"Why is that such a big deal?" Shirley asked. "Barry didn't want to keep the hutch so he let it go with the house. He could have sold the hutch outright, but he didn't. Molly wanted to refinish it. End of story."

Meggie drummed her fingers on the rocking chair and thought about Barry and his reason for not keeping the hutch. Simply stated, he didn't like old furniture. The hutch had no sentimental value to him. It was less work to give it away than try to sell it.

"You're right. I'm making a mountain out of a molehill." Meggie swatted a mosquito on her leg. "Perhaps Molly will refinish it, move it into the house and enjoy it. I think Fred would like that."

Meggie sipped her water and gazed over the front yard. "I suppose he just missed them."

"There you go again." Shirley stopped rocking and turned her body to face her friend. "Who missed what?"

"The documents and old photos Molly found in the hutch." Meggie wrinkled her brow. "I wonder how Barry missed them when he cleaned out the hutch."

"Molly said the photos were bent and the documents faded. She found them crammed behind a drawer. How do you know Barry even cleaned it out?" Shirley's lip curled. "Why are we talking about this anyway?"

Meggie sat up straight. "What if . . ."

"She's on a roll," Shirley muttered mostly to herself.

"What if the old hutch was never meant to leave this farm?" Meggie's eyes bored into Shirley's. "What if, for whatever reason, Fred wanted someone to find those photographs and papers?"

"Oh, yeah." Shirley sighed heavily and threw up her hands. "I'm spending the night with a nut job." Before Meggie could say anything, Shirley rattled on. "If you're so curious about those documents why don't you open the package and read them? It wouldn't be the first time you pried into someone else's business."

"No. We'll drop the box off at the post office in the morning like I promised Molly." Meggie stood up and walked to the edge of the porch. She studied the sky. The sun had hidden behind ominous looking clouds and left in its place a blanket of hot air. It would get dark early. She turned back to Shirley. "If Barry finds something in the papers, it's up to him to investigate. Not me."

"And that's the smartest statement you've made in a long time." Shirley pushed herself to a standing position. "By the way, you never did get around to showing me the hidden staircase. I'm curious."

A diversion couldn't have come at a better time. Meggie motioned Shirley to follow her into the house. In the entryway she reached inside the closet door and found the flashlight. She checked to make sure the batteries were good. "We'll need this. It's dark up there."

Shirley told Meggie to give her a couple minutes and headed for the bathroom. While waiting for her, Meggie decided to take Barry's box out to the Bug. That way she wouldn't forget it. By the time she returned, Shirley stood waiting by the stairway.

CHAPTER 23

ARLY EVENING LIGHT FILTERED through the landing window. "Stairs are going to be the death of me yet." Shirley fanned herself on the way up the stairs.

In the bedroom she gaped at the bookcase. "I would never in a million years suspect this hid a top-secret door. To think I slept up here and never knew anything about it." She shook her shoulders and her face crinkled. "This is all so cloak and dagger, isn't it?"

Meggie agreed and tugged on the bookcase. It groaned, pulled away from the wall and swung open. She pointed out an added feature. A narrow strip of wood ran across the bottom of each shelf to keep the books in place when the door opened.

Shirley stuck her head through the opening and quipped over her shoulder. "You're right. It's dark in here." She stepped back and waved a hand in front of her. "You first, Sherlock. I'll bring up the rear."

Meggie entered the dark area and swept the flashlight around. "Be careful. These stairs are uneven." She bent down in front of the first stair, lifted the tread and shone the light inside.

"So that's where you found the letters? This is so exciting." Shirley ducked under the wall and directed her gaze at the small area under the tread's lid.

Meggie scooted over to make room for Shirley. She shone the light over the cracks along the edges of the wooden bottom. "Why do you suppose Fred left a key in here?"

"Didn't Vera tell you his house had been broken into more than once? Maybe he wanted to hide it just like the letters. Or he might have dropped it there by mistake. Molly said she found it jammed in a crack."

Meggie studied the inside of the hollow stair, ran her finger over the bottom and pushed down on the narrow end. The board flipped up. Her breath hitched. "What in the world?" She reached into the space under the stair's false bottom and lifted out a wooden heart-shaped box. It appeared homemade and a name had been carved across the top. Amelia.

"What do you think this means?"

"I think it means we ask Molly to open the package she wrapped for Barry and take that key out. I'll bet a dollar to a donut hole that's the key to Fred's heart." She set the box under the stair tread until she was through in the attic.

The air had become stifling by the time they reached the top of the stairs. Meggie's forehead dripped with perspiration, her upper lip sprouted beads of sweat. She wiped a hand over her face and ducked into the attic. The same musty smell hung in the air. Low light shone through the only window. "Be careful you don't bump your head," she warned.

Shirley crept through the opening and straightened her posture. "It's completely empty." Her voice echoed in surprise. "There's nothing stored up here."

"That's what made me think Molly and Michael knew nothing about the hidden staircase. They probably thought the trap door in the upstairs bedroom was the only way to the attic. So they stored everything in the garage." Meggie shone the light on the floor in front of her. "Come on. I'll show you the trapdoor."

"Did you hear that?" Shirley stood very still and cocked her ear.

"I didn't hear anything. Your imagination must be playing tricks on you."

"You're probably right, but I would swear someone yelled something. It sounded like it came from that direction." Shirley pointed toward the front of the house. "What happened to that window?"

"I found it broken after the storm and fixed it temporarily." She moved past the trapdoor and pointed it out to Shirley.

"I know I've waffled on whether or not you saw an intruder up here. I want you to know I believe you now."

"Thank you for your vote of confidence." Meggie grinned and strode toward the window. "Come look at the view of the backyard from here."

Shirley edged up to the window. "I just think it's odd that no one seemed to know about the stairway except the intruder."

Meggie gazed out across the backyard, lost in thought. She recalled her first conversation with Amelia Schmidt. "Darrell Schmidt probably knew about the secret passageway. I'm sure he's the mysterious intruder even if he hasn't admitted it."

Shirley tapped her lip. "I wonder why he hasn't come clean."

"Think about it," Meggie explained. "There are repercussions if he admits to breaking and entering. Right now he's being charged with several offenses, but not breaking and entering."

"You're right. He'd get more time in the cooler if they charged him with that."

The evening light faded and a dark veil fell over the farm yard. Meggie turned away from the window. She flashed the light toward the opposite end of the attic. "I think we're done up here. Let's go have dessert."

When Meggie didn't move, Shirley prodded. "What's the matter with you? Why are you standing there? You act like you've seen a ghost or something."

Meggie shaded the flashlight and whispered, "I think I heard the back door slam."

"I didn't hear anything." Shirley looked stricken. "Did we leave the back door unlocked?"

Meggie stepped back and peered out the attic window. She couldn't see anything in the dark, but listened closely. The back door slammed a second time. She put a hand to her chest.

Shirley leaned into her friend. "Maybe Molly came home early."

"No, I don't think it's her. The door slammed twice." Meggie crept to the attic wall. She lowered herself to the floor and pressed her ear over the crack between the attic floor and wall but couldn't hear anything.

Shirley knelt down on all fours next to her. "Are there two of them? What do you think they're up to?" Her voice quivered. "What if they come up to the attic? What are we going to do?"

"I can tell you what we aren't going to do," Meggie whispered. "We aren't going downstairs." She kept her ear to the floor. After several minutes she heard a gruff voice shout, but his words were inaudible. She jabbed her finger toward the opposite end of the attic. "They must be moving through the house."

Shirley gasped and pushed herself up. "They're getting closer. We can't let them know we're up here."

A brief silence came over the house then a female voice bellowed, "Quit arguing. Get the job done or you'll find yourself—"

Before she could finish, a masculine voice cut in, "If I go down you're going with me."

Meggie felt a lump in her throat and swallowed. She pushed herself part-way up. Her leg cramped. She mouthed a scream, rolled over and tried to rub the spasm from her leg.

"Oh, my gosh," Shirley bent over Meggie. "It sounds like they're near the entryway. Try to stand up and walk on your leg." She pulled on her friend's arm.

Meggie fought the pain and stood up. She put weight on both feet. Her hand flew to her mouth. "We left the secret door open."

"We're dead meat," Shirley hissed and glanced around the room. "There's no place to hide."

Meggie put her hands against Shirley's shoulders. "Wait here and don't move." She took the flashlight and limped toward the hidden staircase as quietly as she could.

Once through the opening, she shaded the flashlight and placed her foot on the first stair. She steadied herself against the wall, tapped her way to the second stair. Part way down the flight, her foot slipped. She felt herself falling backward and fought to keep her balance. The flashlight struck the wall.

"What was that? It sounded like it came from upstairs." The man's gravelly voice was barely audible. "I don't think we're alone in the house."

An eerie hush descended. The air grew thick. A stair creaked. Then another. Footsteps grew louder. One footstep sounded heavier than the other. Did the man limp?

Meggie sat on her buttocks and scooted down the remaining stairs. She reached out for the secret door and pulled it towards her.

Footsteps thumped into the bedroom and a rough voice shouted, "You ain't gonna believe this, but I just saw that bookcase move."

"Don't be ridiculous," the woman answered him. "Let's make a quick search up here and leave. She said they're somewhere in the house." The bedroom floor creaked as footsteps shuffled past the secret door and faded.

Meggie stood motionless, elbows pressed into her sides. Only muted sounds broke through the barrier that separated her from danger. She held her hand on her chest to quiet her pounding heart. Something thumped above her. An eerie howl split the air.

"Don't tell me I'm imagining that," the male prowler snarled, his voice growing louder. "I told you, but you wouldn't believe me. I'm out of here. You're on your own. This whole thing was your idea in the first place." Footsteps clumped past the bookcase and down the steps.

"Don't be a fool. There's no such thing as ghosts," the woman called after him. A second set of footsteps rushed past the door. The front door slammed. Footsteps thumped down the stairs. A woman screamed, then a loud thud. A scrambling commotion followed and the front door slammed a second time.

Meggie bowed her head and unclenched her fists. She switched the flashlight on and hurried back up the stairs. She stepped inside the attic and swept the flashlight back and forth. It came to rest on her friend. Her stomach dropped at the sight. Shirley lay sprawled facedown.

She rushed over, knelt down and shook her gently. "Shirley, can you hear me? Where are you hurt?" She flashed the light over the prostrate figure.

Shirley moaned and tried to lift her head. "I'm alive but my head is killing me. I'm not sure all my parts are working." She pushed with her arms to prop herself up. "Are they gone?"

"Yes, they're gone. You scared them off when you fell. They thought you were a ghost."

"If I didn't hurt so much I'd laugh. Am I bleeding?"

Meggie helped her into a sitting position and flashed the light over her face. Her disheveled hair hung over her eyes. Red streaks marked her skin.

"You have a scrape across your forehead. It's barely bleeding, but we better get you downstairs."

Meggie knew she should run downstairs and call the authorities. It seemed heartless to leave her injured friend alone in the attic. The call would have to wait. After a bit of tugging, Meggie managed to get Shirley on her feet. Together they made their way down the stairs.

LATER THAT EVENING after the authorities took their leave, the house was restored to order and all the doors were bolted. Both women had dressed for bed but were in no hurry to retire for the night.

Meggie checked on Brandy and quietly closed the bedroom door. She joined Shirley at the kitchen table. A cool breeze blew through the open window along with the gentle pitter-patter of rain. Nature's way of soothing nerves.

"I wonder what they were looking for." Shirley spooned a bite of marble cake and vanilla ice cream into her mouth.

"I don't have any idea, but I'm pretty sure they didn't find it. And from the way they took off, I don't think they cared." Meggie twirled the spoon in her ice cream. "I did tell the deputy that it sounded like the male intruder limped. I mentioned my suspicions about Simon. Maybe that information will help."

"What did Molly say when you told her about the intruders?"

"She took the news hard. She wanted to come home right away, but I told her we would hold the fort down. There's nothing she could do if she did come home."

Shirley finished her dessert and pushed the plate aside. "Remember when we first went up to the attic and I told you I heard someone yell? I don't think I imagined that. But why would they let us know they were here to rob the place?"

Meggie seemed lost in thought for several seconds. "Now that you mention it, I remember a couple years back when a customer came into the shop. She told a strange story.

Shirley pulled her chair closer to the table and propped her chin on her hand. "Nothing you can tell me will seem strange anymore. Spit it out."

Meggie cleared her throat. "At the time she lived in the country not far from Pine Lake. It was during the summer. Evidently, she had been reading but grew tired and decided to call it a night. She set her book on the bedside table and turned the light off. She started to doze when she heard the front doorbell ring."

"At first she thought it was her imagination playing tricks on her. Who would be visiting so late at night? But when the doorbell rang a second time she crawled out of bed and went to answer the door."

"She peeked through the small window in the door but couldn't see anyone."

"You mean there was no one there? I bet some neighborhood kids were out pulling pranks. Somebody's little angels had nothing better to do than ring doorbells late at night and take off running."

Meggie shook her head. "The doorbell rang again so my neighbor inched the door open. Two young girls about eight or nine years old stood on the steps under the porch light with umbrellas extended in their hands."

Shirley frowned. "What in the world were two young girls doing out so late at night?"

"That was the first thought that crossed her mind. The fact that it wasn't raining was the next thought to cross her mind." Meggie paused and pushed her ice cream away. "One of the young girls asked the woman if she had seen their dog. But when the woman questioned them about the dog's description, they didn't answer her. They backed away from the door, turned and ran down the sidewalk out of sight."

"That's strange. Why would two young girls ring a doorbell late at night, ask about their lost dog, and not wait around for an answer?" Shirley threw up her hands. "Not to mention they had umbrellas when it wasn't raining."

"I didn't understand it at first either. But after thinking about it for a while, it all made sense. The whole thing was a ruse to find out if anyone was at home. I'm sure someone must have been waiting for those young girls on the road."

"And if the girls reported no one at home, the burglary would be good to go." A blank look crossed Shirley's face. "What about the umbrellas?"

Meggie smiled. "The woman couldn't describe the girls because the porch light shone down on the umbrellas and shaded their faces."

Shirley scratched her jaw. "That's quite a story and it all makes perfect sense." She looked at Meggie. "What are you frowning about?"

"I just remembered the female prowler said, 'She said they're somewhere in the house.'" Meggie thought a minute. "Who was she and what was she talking about?"

Shirley yawned, lightly slapped the table with her hand and stood up. "Now you're talking riddles. I think I'm going to turn in. It's been a long day." Her eyes roved over the table. "By the way, where is that package you were going to mail for Molly?"

"In the car along with the carton of tomatoes she gave us. I didn't want to forget them in the morning."

After Shirley retired to bed, Meggie sat alone with her thoughts. The pieces of the puzzle were beginning to fit together, but the biggest piece was still missing. Who killed Fred?

If she knew all the players in this mystery she might figure out who murdered Fred and why. Until that time, his spirit wouldn't rest and neither would she.

CHAPTER 24

MEGGIE SPENT A GOOD DEAL of August at Hearts and Flowers Gift Shop. More tourists than usual invaded Pine Lake in August. Eldon still wore the cast on his leg, which limited his ability to work. And while Vera arrived early and left late, she devoted a significant amount of time to wedding plans.

One Friday morning Meggie arrived with a bouquet of pink, red and white painted daisies. Vera oohed and aahed and suggested she find a vase in the breakroom. "Please bring them out front so the customers can enjoy them as well. There's nothing like a colorful bouquet of flowers to brighten up one's day."

Meggie disappeared behind the breakroom curtain and came back a couple minutes later. She set the floral arrangement on the end of the counter, sidled up to Vera and looked over her shoulder. "You've been busy, I see."

"I arrived in the wee hours this morning and have been working on our wedding plans ever since. The park will be a lovely location for a wedding." Vera glowed. "And the large gazebo will provide shelter if the weather doesn't cooperate. We won't plan on many guests. Just a few close friends. Maybe some quiet music." She glanced outside. "I do hope this weather holds."

Meggie recalled Vera's hesitation when several acquaintances suggested she consider an outdoor wedding in Pine Lake Park and invite her close friends. It took a fair amount of coaxing on their part and careful consideration on Vera's before she decided it would be a splendid idea. Eldon readily agreed.

"I'm so glad you changed your mind and decided against a private ceremony."

"We couldn't be happier about the change in plans. Our dear friends will be with us on our special day. In the whole scheme of things that's what really matters."

Meggie patted Vera's arm. "If you need help with anything you be sure to let me know."

The bell tinkled above the door and the first customer of the day stepped into the shop. A smile lit up Vera's face. She tucked her wedding plans under the counter. "Good morning, Detective Peterson."

Meggie pasted a smile on her face, stepped out from behind the counter and asked if she could help him find something. She took in Bulldog's street clothes and sensed his unease. "Are you looking for anything in particular?"

"Actually, I'm shopping for my mother's birthday present." Bulldog confided that his mother's eyesight had deteriorated to a point where small print had become too difficult to read. "A friend told me he bought a cookbook here in large print. I'd like to take a look at one if you have any left."

"I believe we do." Meggie lifted the cookbook from the book rack and handed it to Bulldog. She rotated the rack. "We had a dessert cookbook in large print, too, but I see it's no longer here." She nodded at the cookbook in Bulldog's hand. "But there's a variety of dessert recipes in that cookbook."

While Meggie discussed cookbooks her mind wandered to Fred Jackson's investigation. She felt the urge to question Bulldog about it but didn't know how to broach the subject.

"My mother still loves to cook and fixes me a home-cooked meal every week. She insists I keep my strength up so I'm able to catch the bad guys." Bulldog grinned. He turned the book over and checked the price. His face fell. "Little spendy for a bunch of recipes, isn't it?"

"You won't be able to find many cookbooks in large print. Your mother will really appreciate your thoughtfulness." Meggie stood by until he made his decision to buy it then followed him to the card rack. "Speaking of bad guys, have you had any luck finding the person responsible for Fred's death?"

Bulldog hesitated, gave her a sidelong glance and chuckled. "That's a loaded question. You know I can't talk about the case, but I can tell you we're working on it."

He spun the card rack until he came to those cards marked half-off, picked one out and clumped over to the counter. He laid the cookbook and card down and pulled his wallet from his back pocket. "Do you gift wrap by chance?"

Meggie moved behind the counter and conveyed to him that there would be an extra charge for gift wrapping. When Bulldog shook his head she pointed out the gift bag selection near the card rack. In the end he decided to wrap it at home and handed over his money.

She slipped Bulldog's purchases into a bag and thanked him for stopping. She watched him walk out to his truck and tapped a finger against her lip. How much wasn't he telling her? Surely by this time they had someone of interest in Fred's case.

It was common knowledge that Darrell Schmidt finally admitted to breaking and entering Riley's house to search the attic. But he still denied having anything to do with Fred's death.

Donna, Riley's nosy neighbor, stated she had seen Fred the day Darrell was arrested. If that were true, Darrell couldn't have harmed Fred.

The identity of the two intruders at the farmhouse still remained a mystery. At the time, she couldn't be sure who the intruders were or what they were looking for in the Rileys' home.

But the next day after she dropped the package off at the post office and returned home, she did a fair amount of reflection. It dawned on her that the documents and photographs might have been the object of their search.

Perhaps there was something among the photographs and documents someone didn't want Barry to see. But who knew about Molly's discovery besides Molly, Michelle, and Barry? It made no sense that either Michelle or Barry would break into the farmhouse to steal something that belonged to Barry. Perhaps Michelle mentioned the box to her mother.

It was pure conjecture on her part that the intruders were looking for the photographs and documents, but nevertheless she had called Bulldog with her suspicions. Whether he acted on them or not she didn't know.

Meggie's musings came to an end when a group of ladies walked through the door of Hearts and Flowers. They chattered on their way through the shop, past the candles and stopped near the mosaics display. A few minutes after they arrived they walked out with several purchases.

Customers were in and out of the shop the rest of the afternoon. Vera had no time to spend on wedding plans. She looked forward to visiting Eldon after work to go over wedding arrangements.

By the end of the day Meggie looked forward to spending a quiet evening at home with Walter. Even if he sat in front of the television while she sat on the deck, they would still be home together.

LATER THAT MONTH, the wedding day arrived with sunny skies and a hint of fall in the air. Pine Lake Park buzzed with activity. Since Vera had been reluctant to have a bridal shower, her friends insisted on decorating and providing the wedding feast.

Vera had readily agreed to their offer to decorate but hesitated over the potluck idea. She didn't think it proper for her guests to bring food to the wedding. But at everyone's insistence she soon relented.

Meggie arrived early to help decorate and prepare the gazebo and reception area for the grand occasion. Shortly after, Shirley and Molly joined her. The three women were busy arranging flowers in the park shelter when a loud roar sounded close by.

Vera's cousin, Nettie, had arrived on the scene. The plump woman emerged from the driver's seat of the car and walked around to the passenger side. She plopped a straw hat on her head, pulled a large tray from the vehicle and strode towards the park shelter.

"Hello, ladies," she crooned and set her homemade dinner rolls off to the side. She surveyed the entire shelter. Her eyes came to rest on the eight-foot table the three women had wiped down. "We'll have this table set in no time. It'll make a wonderful food table."

Nettie spread a white plastic covering over the large rectangular table and laid her handmade white-lace tablecloth on top of it. While walking the perimeter of the table, she tugged the tablecloth to make sure it hung evenly. Satisfied, she gave the high sign to Molly and Shirley to begin setting the buffet table.

By the time the last guest arrived, the table overflowed with an array of foods. Hotdishes, cold salads, and baked beans along with an assortment of breads spread out over the festive tabletop. A vase of fresh flowers at the end of the table added the finishing touch.

Audrey Peterson arrived at the last minute with a wedding cake, compliments of Swenson's bakery. She set it down near the flowers and tossed a number of rose petals around it.

Sprigs of greenery hung over the gazebo's entrance and fresh flowers were visible inside the building. Eldon's nephew strummed soft guitar music in the background.

A rose garden stood a distance from the summerhouse. While the flowers were no longer at their peak, the rockery surrounding the garden and the water fountain lent a romantic air to the occasion.

Meggie looked over the crowd gathered for the wedding. She waved to Molly Riley as the young woman slipped into a seat at the end of her row. Molly held her camera up and smiled.

At last the moment arrived. Vera and Eldon stood in front of the minister and recited their vows. When they were finished the clergyman presented the couple. "Now you may kiss the bride."

Applause rose and contagious smiles spread all around. Eldon leaned over, Vera puckered up and somewhere in the crowd a cell phone rang. Heads turned as Molly sprang to her feet. She grabbed her purse and hurried away from the gathering.

Walter nudged his wife and nodded to the congratulations line. When Meggie's turn came to offer her congratulations, she hugged both Vera and Eldon and wished them the best. She felt a tap on her shoulder and turned to find Molly by her side, a dazed look on her face.

"Barry just called. The authorities have made arrests in Fred's murder."

CHAPTER 25

I STILL CAN'T BELIEVE I WON a free weekend for two at the new bed and breakfast on Shadow Lake." Meggie fastened her seatbelt and leaned back in the passenger seat of Walter's pickup truck. "We're actually going to spend some time together for a change." She winked at her husband. "It might be kind of romantic."

"You act like we're never together when in reality we're seldom apart. Except, of course," Walter raised his hand in the air, "when you're off on one of your housesitting adventures involved in murder and mayhem." He winked back at her.

"I'll admit you are right on one point. I am beginning to wonder if I should housesit anymore." Meggie gazed out the truck's window and thought about the recent close calls she had while housesitting.

She shuddered and told herself it wouldn't do any good to cry over spilt milk. Instead she would focus on the fall scenery and the exciting weekend ahead. But try as she might, her mind kept wandering back to the hobby farm and Fred's ghost.

For some time she couldn't figure out why his ghost sought her out and not Molly or Michael. It baffled her, but after some deliberation she concluded that while Molly and Michael were permanent residents in the house, she had been curious and discovered Fred's remains.

"It's hard to believe the mystery surrounding Fred's death ended the way it did." Meggie spoke in a low voice. "I'm glad it's all over. To think Barry Jackson's ex-wife planned the murder while she was still married to him. And she hired her brother to commit the crime. How cold is that?"

"She waved money in front of Simon's face and he jumped at the chance to do her bidding." Walter shook his head. "And after all

Fred did for him, helped him out when he needed it. That's what greed does to a person."

"Jacqueline Jackson used her head when she planned the divorce and the murder," Meggie added. "She waited until after the deed to ask Barry for a divorce. That way she could cash in on the farm. Obviously, she didn't want to wait around for Fred to die."

"Greed again," Walter said. "And they almost got away with it."

Meggie thought about the documents that turned up in the old hutch. Fred kept contracts on the jobs he hired out. Simon had contracted to fill the old well. Simon bided his time, waited for the right opportunity to get rid of Fred. When that opportunity arose, he took it. He had strangled Fred and tossed him down the well. Then literally covered up his crime.

All those years he probably worried about someone finding the contract. But it was another piece of evidence the authorities found that would nail his coffin shut. A pair of eyeglasses found at the bottom of the well. The same odd prescription as the eyeglasses he purchased soon after Fred went missing. And the photo of Simon wearing the taped up glasses made it official.

"I wish I could have been a fly on the wall when he sang like a canary and pointed the finger at his sister."

Meggie shook her head to free her mind of cobwebs and shaded her eyes against the sun. According to her calculations they were more than half way to their destination.

Walter turned off the highway onto a county road. The truck rolled past rows of yellowed cornstalks and empty vegetable stands. Further on two men baled grass hay. The grind and squeal of machinery split the air then faded as the truck sped by.

She closed her eyes, thought about the fleeting summer and inhaled the fresh scent of autumn. "Nothing is going to spoil this weekend," she vowed more to herself than to Walter.

"The weekend I will enjoy. It's the murder mystery dinner I'm not so sure about."

Meggie laughed and thought about the character descriptions they received in the mail from the staff at Shadow Lake Bed and Breakfast. She looked forward to the mystery dinner on Saturday night, but Walter didn't share her enthusiasm.

She reached over and tickled his neck. "It's going to be fun. It's not every day you get to dress up in costume. And you're going to be lord of an old English manor where murder and mayhem run rampant."

"Murder and mayhem are more your style than mine." Walter peeked at Meggie from the corner of his eye. "I don't understand why you want to pretend murder and mayhem when you've been through the real deal more times than I care to remember."

She couldn't argue with him on that point, so she chose to say nothing and settled back to enjoy the surrounding countryside. The road wound through a colorful neighborhood of trees touched by warm autumn days and cool nights.

The birch tree's golden leaves shimmered in the sun while fiery red maple leaves glowed nearby. Peppered along the road on both sides were impressive oaks. Their branches reached for the sky to show off their reddish-brown leaves. The pines held fast to their deep green color.

They drove on and soon the landscape changed. Patches of blue peeked through clusters of pine trees then transformed into a choppy body of water, its waves capped in white.

"Is that Shadow Lake?" Meggie's body posture perked up.

"I believe so." Walter leaned forward, his eyes squinted. "Yes, there's the sign. Shadow Lake. Now let's watch for the fire number of the B & B. I think we're close."

"I hope the wind dies down by tomorrow or no boating for us." She knew her husband would be disappointed if the weather didn't cooperate this weekend. He had been thrilled when she told him the weekend included use of watercraft. "The forecast said sunny skies and unusually warm September weather for the weekend. Right now it's seems to be cooling off." She rolled the passenger window partway up and slipped her sweater on.

"I might even try a speed boat if they have one." Walter leaned forward and rushed his words, "I know it's too cold for a jet ski but a speed boat will do."

A sign on the right side of the road announced Shadow Lake Bed and Breakfast. Walter slowed the truck and turned into the narrow paved drive. The private road sloped around several tall pine trees and ended in front of an imposing two-story house.

Meggie leaned forward in her seat. "What a beautiful house. It looks just like the pictures I've seen of old English manors. Oh, and look at those quaint cabins."

Walter pulled up in the parking area and braked the truck. He crawled out, hoisted the piece of luggage over the back end of the vehicle and wheeled it to the front of the truck. He turned to Meggie and offered his arm. "Shall we, my dear?"

Meggie linked her arm in his. Together they made their way down a brick-lined path to the main entrance of the house, followed by the *click clack* of rolling luggage. She held the door for her husband and followed him into the house.

A grand fireplace stood off to the left with a black grate filled with firewood next to it. The scent of lemon oil wafted in the air. The oak floors gleamed. Beyond the fireplace a staircase wound gracefully to the upper floor.

Antique furnishings displayed throughout the room lent a glimpse of another era. Meggie stopped next to an old fashioned writing desk, lifted the feather pen and signed their names in the guest book.

At the check-in area a petite middle-aged woman welcomed them and handed Walter a key to the room. She asked if they needed help with their luggage, but Walter declined the offer.

"You'll be staying in Pearl's Room, the largest suite on the second floor. It is our loveliest room. We're so pleased the Pine Lake Lions Club chose Shadow Lake Bed and Breakfast as grand prize in their drawing."

Upstairs, Meggie stepped into a charming room. A rose-patterned bedspread covered a queen-sized bed that graced the center of the room. Matching curtains hung to the side of an enormous window that faced Shadow Lake.

The top portion of the bedroom walls were papered in a subdued rose pattern with the bottom portion wainscoted. In one corner of the room sat a table for two where guests could enjoy a cup of tea or coffee and gaze out over the blue water.

LATER THAT EVENING, MEGGIE dressed for dinner in a teal-colored dress and slipped on her favorite pair of heels. She glanced in the mirror, fluffed her hair and called to Walter. "I'm ready when you are." When he didn't answer she peeked out of the bathroom. He stood in front of the picture window and appeared transfixed by Shadow Lake.

She joined him at the window and took in the lovely view. Impressive pines framed the spectacle, sentinels over the great body of water. The setting sun cast a shine over the rolling waves. In gentle rhythm they rose and fell until at the end of their journey they lapped against the shore and disappeared forever.

"Look," Meggie pointed. "The wooden stairs go all the way down to the beach." She slipped her arm around Walter and peeked up at him. "How does a romantic walk after dinner sound?"

Walter agreed with the idea and suggested she take an outer wrap to dinner since the evening might turn chilly. He bent down and pecked her on the cheek. "Madam, I do believe it is time for dinner."

After they had eaten dinner, the Moores made their way down the wooden steps to the beach. When they reached the last stair, Meggie pulled her shawl tight around her shoulders, knotted it loosely and hooked her arm with Walter's. They strolled for a distance until they happened onto a log bench that faced the lake and looked inviting.

Meggie pulled her shoes off and set them on the ground beside the bench. She sat down next to Walter, tucked her feet under her and laid her head on his shoulder. A gentle breeze blew off the lake.

Its breath rippled the moonlit path on the black water. "Did you know there's a legend about a lost treasure in Shadow Lake? I read about it in a pamphlet I picked up in the lobby."

"You're kidding. Lost treasure in Shadow Lake?" Walter wrapped his arm around his wife's shoulder. "I've heard of lost treasure at sea but never in a lake. Sounds like a big story to lure tourists to Shadow Lake." He patted her arm. "But then, you believe that lakes in Minnesota were formed when Paul Bunyan's boot tracks filled with rainwater."

"Don't make fun." Meggie snuggled up to Walter. "I think it sounds exciting."

"Excitement seems to be your middle name."

No one said anything for a while. Then Meggie broke into laughter.

Walter wrinkled his nose. "What's so funny?"

"I'm sorry. But I keep thinking about how Jacqueline and Simon tore out of the farmhouse the night they searched for that box of documents." She paused. "Shirley still has no idea why she tripped. Maybe Fred's ghost had something to do with it. If she hadn't fallen, who knows what would have happened to us."

Walter pointed up at the stars. "You never know. Fred might be smiling down on us right now and giving us the high sign."

Following a few moments of silence Meggie said, "Talk about romantic."

"You mean us?" Walter stroked her arm.

"No. I mean Fred and Amelia." Meggie thought about the letter and the ring Fred left inside the wooden heart. "He promised to help Amelia through a divorce and marry her." She stared down at her own wedding ring. "To think they came so close to finding true happiness."

"I imagine it was bittersweet for Amelia when she opened the wooden heart."

The evening wore on. Scattered clouds floated over the moon and the sparkling path across the water faded. The breeze had turned to a gusty wind.

"Well, Mrs. Moore, shall we call it a night?" Walter's shoulders shook. "And get romantic?"

THE NEXT EVENING THE MOORES lingered over drinks in the dining room. One candle flickered in the center of their table. Meggie reached for her husband's hand and squeezed it. "I thought you made the perfect Lord of the Manor." Her eyes crinkled. "Even if you turned out to be a cold-blooded killer."

Walter grinned and puffed out his chest. "I have to admit I acted way beyond my expectations. Of course, that's not saying much since I had no expectations."

"I see you two seem to be enjoying yourselves." Shelby Taylor, owner of Shadow Lake Bed and Breakfast edged up to the table. The tall distinguished-looking woman turned to Walter. "I hear you were quite the addition to the mystery dinner tonight."

Walter seemed somewhat embarrassed by the praise. He thanked her for the compliment and admitted he enjoyed the event.

"Don't forget. We have a delectable breakfast in the morning that you won't want to miss."

After she walked away, Walter glanced at his watch and suggested they head up to their room. "I've had a lot of fun this weekend. We should do this more often."

THE NEXT MORNING MEGGIE and Walter finished breakfast and were enjoying a cup of coffee when Shelby Taylor sought them out. "May I sit down for a moment?" she asked.

When they both invited her to join them, she lowered herself into a chair.

"I don't want to impose so I'll come right to the point. I just received a phone call from my son who lives in Billings. He announced that he's getting married in June." She laid her hand on the table and looked at Meggie. "We are going to need someone to look after the bed and breakfast for a short period of time while we attend the wedding."

Walter bumped his water glass, but grabbed it before it tipped.

"A Lion's Club member told me you housesit on occasion and highly recommended you. Our main concern is that we have someone here to oversee the day-to-day business, make sure everything stays on schedule. Our staff is most dependable, so I don't anticipate any problems. We want to know we're leaving our B & B in good hands."

Walter's eyes bored into Meggie's. He mumbled something about his wife having second thoughts about housesitting.

"Please think about it, won't you? Be sure to pick up a business card before you leave. It has all our contact information on it." She turned to Walter. "If Meggie decides to housesit for us next summer, you are more than welcome to join her."

After they returned to their suite, Walter paced back and forth. "You admitted on the drive here you were unsure whether or not you wanted to housesit anymore. I hope you use your head and tell Shelby Taylor no."

Meggie hated to see a wonderful getaway end on a sour note. She didn't need to make a decision today. She could think about it, weigh the pros and cons, and then decide. She was a big girl. She didn't need her husband to think for her.

THE NEXT MORNING WALTER handed the room key to Shelby Taylor. He thanked her for the hospitality, dropped his gaze to the business cards displayed on the counter and quickly looked away.

Meggie shook Shelby's hand, praised the bed and breakfast but made no mention of the housesitting request. She smiled at Walter and nodded. As he turned to go, she reached behind him and picked up a Shadow Lake Bed and Breakfast business card. She tucked it into her purse, glanced up at Shelby and winked.

Acknowledgments

Thank you to Angela Foster, editor, and North Star Press. A special thanks to Five Wings Arts Council for awarding me grants, with funds from the McKnight Foundation supplemented with Legacy funds, to further my knowledge of writing.